NOTHING LASTS FOREVER

Loretta Miles Tollefson

PALO FLECHADO PRESS

Other Books by Loretta Miles Tollefson

Locke Family Saga
Not Just Any Man
Not My Father's House
No Secret Too Small

Other Old New Mexico Fiction
There Will Be Consequences
The Texian Prisoners
An Unhappy Country
The Pain and The Sorrow

Old One Eye Pete (short stories)
Valley of the Eagles (micro fiction)

Other Fiction
The Ticket
The Streets of Seattle

Poetry
But Still My Child
And Then Moses Was There
Mary at the Cross

For Lowell, because Alma is still his favorite.

EPIGRAPH

No hay mal qué siempre dure, ni bien qué nunca acabe.

There is no wrong that lasts forever and no happiness that cannot end.

Dichos, Proverbs, and Sayings from the Spanish
Charles Aranda

NOTHING LASTS FOREVER

Loretta Miles Tollefson

ALMA

CHAPTER 1 – SUMMER 1843
Moreno Valley, New Mexico

Alma sits on a flat sandstone boulder in the long grass beside her grandfather's grave and studies the long mountain valley below. Her father and brother are in the hay meadow, hunting prairie dogs. Ramón, her godfather and her father's business partner, leads a horse from the steep-roofed adobe-and-log barn to the small forge between it and the log cabin. The forge her Grandfather Locke built and tended so carefully.

Tears well in Alma's eyes. She pushes her overly curly black hair away from her light brown face. She has never believed the old adage that death is a part of life, a natural occurrence. It's always seemed more of a tearing to her, a ragged hole in the fabric of life.

She lays her hand on Grandfather Locke's sun-warmed headstone. Her mother is ill. She lies in the cabin on the hillside below, thinner than ever, with no energy for her loom, her plants, or her cornfield. Chaser IV, the big brown mastiff named for his three predecessors, is crouched on the floor beside the bed instead of patrolling the crops against deer and raccoons. He is bereft without the woman to guide him.

As is the girl. Alma lifts her tearstained face. The clouds above the mountains on the other side of the valley won't devolve into rain until late this evening. How beautiful they are, with the sun shining above them like that. How oddly steady. She takes a deep breath, absorbing them, the mountains, and the hillside beneath her, the fall grasses soft under her hand. Surely her mother will get well and become her active, opinionated self once again.

Movement flickers on the dusty track that runs north-south down the center of the valley. A man and a horse, both walking. Alma squints, then grins. The man is wearing a black cassock, his bulky shoulders at aggressive odds with the priestly garment. The fact that he's walking beside his mount is another sign. It's Padre Antonio José Martínez, the perpetually restless Catholic priest from Taos. Has he heard that her mother is sick and walked east thirty miles to try once again to convert her?

Alma chuckles, stands, and bats grass seeds from her skirt. Her mother may be ill, but there's nothing wrong with her tongue. This should be fun to watch.

But when the padre arrives, he has more than conversion on his mind. After the usual greetings and offers of food and drink, he gets down to business.

"¡Los americanos!" he grumbles, his high forehead creased with indignation.

Suzanna has risen and dressed in honor of his visit. Her rocking chair tilts to a stop as he speaks, and her dark eyes sharpen in her tired face. "What was that?"

"Not you," Martínez says hastily. "You are one of us, your mother was half Navajo. And you," he turns to Alma's father, Gerald. "You have your own reasons for never returning to the land that would enslave you."

Gerald's gray eyes smile noncommittally as Suzanna frowns. The priest turns to Alma and her curly haired blond brother, Andrew, who are side by side on the bench by the corner bookcase. "It's that americano trader, Charles Bent. He's the worst kind of American. Greedy, arrogant—" He trails off, then swings back to their parents. "His ambitions will affect you now. He's taking the land from under your feet!"

Gerald frowns. "Has Bent become involved in the land grant Governor Armijo gave to Guadalupe Miranda and Carlos Beaubien two years ago?"

The priest nods. His scowl deepens. "I thought my arguments then had effectively blocked that travesty of justice, but Armijo is back in power again and he's approved their request despite all my protests and objections. Yes, we are under Mexican law now, but the amount he's granted them is three times what would have been allowed under the Spanish! Almost two hundred thousand of your American acres!"

He waves an arm toward the door. "It includes all the land east of the mountain ridges on the west side of this valley." Then he waves toward the opposite wall. "And everything beyond, the Cimarron River and all that drains into it. Vast amounts of timber and unspoiled grasslands. Almost everything the people of Taos Pueblo have hunted and grazed for generations! It's part of their original grant from the Spanish crown! All Taos is enraged!" He nods at Suzanna. "Your father agrees with me, but even his words didn't sway Manuel Armijo."

"I suppose the Governor is worried that the U.S. will move into it and take anything that isn't clearly occupied," she says.

"Then he should send out colonists he can trust! People Beaubien and Miranda have chosen! But not Bent, that pretentious, greedy, spite-tongued Missouri merchant! They gave him the right to twenty-five percent of the grant, and you can be sure he'll use his portion to control it all in the end!" He shakes a finger at her. "This will not end well, for you or anyone else!"

Gerald stirs uneasily. "I expect it'll work out in the long run. It's a great deal of land."

"More than any of them have a right to!"

"There's room enough for us all."

The priest sniffs disparagingly and shakes his head. Suzanna glances at her husband with a slight frown. He nods. "I'll talk it over with Ramón."

"That is all I can ask," Padre Martínez says. He rises from his seat and bows courteously, then turns to Alma. "I'd like to pray at the grave of your grandfather, if you will take me to it." He turns his big head toward her mother. "He was un buen hombre, good although still a Protestant."

Suzanna and Alma exchange a grin as the girl leads the priest toward the door.

When she returns to the cabin, Andrew has disappeared into the marsh below the house, where the Cimarron River begins, and her parents are on the porch. Suzanna, weak as she is, paces restlessly while Gerald sits on the wooden bench by the door, gazing at the mountains on the other side of the valley.

"We need that paper," Suzanna says.

"I'll talk to Carlos Beaubien the next time we're in Taos."

"And when will that be? This fall? Next year?"

He studies the fields below. "It depends on the harvest." Then he looks up at the mountains again. The clouds are lower now, a wave of moisture creating a screen of gray mist over the pines on the lower slopes. "And how soon winter arrives. Ramón says it may come early this year."

She scowls at him and turns away, stalking to the other end of the porch. She turns to make another pass, then suddenly jerks sideways and grabs at the railing. Alma and Gerald both start toward her, but she waves them away. "It was just a spasm. It's already over." She frowns at Alma, as if registering her presence for the first time. "Where is the padre? Did he leave without saying goodbye?"

"He's still at the gravesite."

Suzanna nods and absently rubs her side, then looks down the hill toward the rows of corn shining green in the sun. "I should check for critter damage." She looks around. "Where's Chaser?"

A dog barks as if in answer and the big mastiff lopes from the hillside behind the barn as Ramón emerges from the building, leading the padre's horse. The priest moves toward him while the dog trots to the house. Suzanna sinks to the steps to greet him.

Padre Martínez and the old man exchange a few words, then the priest swings into his saddle and guides his mount to the porch. He raises a hand in benediction. "I bid you farewell and good health," he says formally.

Suzanna grins up at him mischievously. "I feel better already."

TERESINA

CHAPTER 2 – CIRCA 1880
Taos, New Mexico

I am old now, and I give the journalists what they want to hear. A narrative of whole cloth, moving past the jagged remnants of memory, the shards of a once colorful clay pot on the hard-packed floor of my childhood.

That day in late May 1846, when my half sister Rumalda was married, may be my last truly happy recollection. She was not a particularly pretty girl—her long wavy hair was her only true glory—but her flushed face and bright eyes glowed with happiness as my father placed her hand on Tomás Boggs' arm.

I stood next to my mother, whose cheeks were marked with tears even as she smiled. "So young," she whispered, squeezing my hand.

I looked up at her. Rumalda was fifteen, ten years older than I was. She had always seemed very mature to me, on a par with my mother's beautiful sister, Josefa. Josefa was married. Why shouldn't Rumalda be, also?

And the round-faced Tomás Boggs was a kind man, even if his lank hair was often in his face. He liked children and often brought my siblings and me candy. And he always called my hair "auburn" instead of "red." He and Josefa's husband, Christopher Carson, were good friends.

So, I didn't understand my mother's tears that day. Certainly, my father, Charles Bent, was happy. Normally a reserved and somewhat cynical man, his thin face beamed with delight as he moved among our guests. He even went so far as to clap some of the men on the back and bow to the old ladies. He had an extra smile for the Lashones, the couple whose house shared our back wall. He didn't always get along with them but today was different. He would let bygones be bygones.

However, he was still an unbending man, and he didn't go so far as to extend any pleasantries to Padre Martínez, who'd been invited by Tomás and cajoled by Josefa into performing the ceremony.

The priest was in a far corner, sipping punch and listening impatiently while my godfather, Don Cornelio, told a story. Normally, Mother might have been concerned about keeping the two men apart, but today she was focused on my father, watching him with a fond smile.

"He seems content with the match," Luis Lee said from behind us. "Even though Boggs is a mere employee of the Bent and Saint Vrain business firm."

Mama turned toward the tall man with the long blond hair and weak chin. "Tomás is Charles' trusted friend and the son of Missouri's former governor," she said. "We are both quite pleased."

"Ah, so there are political considerations, as well." When she frowned at him, he shrugged. "The connection will be useful before long. I expect everyone in Taos will be American citizens before the year is out, whether they want to be or not."

Her smile dropped. She reached for my shoulder, as if anchoring herself. "So, you also believe los americanos will invade?"

He nodded toward my father, who now stood near the corner fireplace, speaking to Tomás and Ceran Saint Vrain. "Doesn't he?"

"So he tells me." She glanced toward Padre Martínez. Worry lines marred her forehead. "Charles is confident in your American military prowess, but I foresee confusion and conflict and trouble. And until the invasion—if it occurs—does take place, foreigners here could suffer confiscation of property and other outrages."

Her eyes swept the room and landed on Rumalda beside the fireplace, smiling happily as Josefa made a slight adjustment to her skirt. Mother's chin lifted. She looked up at Luis Lee. "However, those are only possible troubles. Today is a day to celebrate certain joy and new beginnings." Then she frowned. "I do wish Christopher was here."

"Carson and Lucien Maxwell are still off in California with John Fremont?"

She nodded absently. I pressed her hand. "Father will make sure we are safe," I said confidently.

Don Luis' head swung toward me and both adults smiled indulgently. "Yes, your father will protect us," Mama said as Señor Lee patted her arm and moved away.

On the other end of the room, the violinists father had hired began to play, and my brother and sister moved into position for the first dance. Estefina had recently grown several inches and was now taller than nine-year-old Alfredo, even though she was younger by two years. They looked a little ridiculous.

But then Mama said, "Come! It is a day for celebration. Rumalda is married!" and my godfather came toward me, his hands out in an invitation to dance.

- 9 -

ALMA

CHAPTER 3 – JUNE 1846
Moreno Valley, New Mexico

Footsteps thud on the wooden floor outside the bedroom door, past the loom. Suzanna hands the empty broth cup back to Alma and smiles faintly. "That will be your brother." They grin at each other. Andrew is a quiet boy with a heavy step. The incongruity is a family joke he doesn't find amusing.

There's a tap on the door. Alma rises and opens it.

"Is she awake?" His brown eyes are anxious and excited at the same time. When Alma nods, he leans into the room. "Someone's coming up the valley. A whole passel of people."

Suzanna pushes at the blankets and sits up. "I expect it's Stands Alone and his family."

He shakes his head. "They have wagons. And cows. And someone real tall is leading the way."

She frowns at him. "Quite tall, or very tall. Not 'real.'"

He grins and pushes his curly blond hair away from his sand-brown face. "Extremely tall. And wide, as well. Ramón thinks it's probably Ceran Saint Vrain."

She gestures to Alma and moves her legs toward the edge of the bed. "I need to dress."

* * * *

Ceran Saint Vrain smiles at Alma as he takes a sugar-dusted biscochito from the platter she offers him. Her curly black hair still smells of woodsmoke from the fire she started as Ramón mixed the dough. "You have been quite industrious," he teases. His eyes drift to the dark heart-shaped mark on her cheek and he smiles slightly. "Have you learned to bake since we last met?"

Beside him, Charles Bent laughs as her father chuckles, his gray eyes twinkling. "She is helpful in more ways than baking," he says.

Andrew circles the room, refilling glasses and cups with water and coffee. Ramón comes from the kitchen and leans toward Suzanna's rocking chair. He says something in her ear, and she smiles up at him gratefully. Then she turns to the woman beside her. "You have travelled far today?"

The woman looks at her in confusion, and Suzanna switches to Spanish. "¿Ha viajado lejos hoy?"

The woman smiles and nods and rattles off an answer as Alma proffers the cookies. The woman's eyes move politely over Alma's face, but don't react to the dark splotches on her forehead or the heart-shaped mark on her cheek. Instead, she explains that the little group of settlers left Taos two days ago. She and the other women have never been this far into the mountains. She was glad to see that it's possible to build a house here, even if it isn't made of adobe.

Suzanna laughs and says she was uncomfortable living in a log house when she first arrived but has grown used to it.

"You will have an adobe if you prefer it," Saint Vrain tells the woman. He glances at her husband, who watches them all without speaking. "That is, if tu esposo agrees."

The other man shrugs. "It is as you wish."

"As you yourself wish, man!" Charles Bent leans forward, his narrow, perpetually skeptical face suddenly alight. "You'll have land of your own and space for as many buildings as you can construct, adobe or log! The Poñil and the valley of the Cimarron contain everything you need!"

The man smiles thinly. Gerald raises an eyebrow. "The valley of the Cimarron? How far up the canyon are you settling these people?"

"Oh, far enough down, where the land opens up. Mostly around Poñil Creek. Though some of them may want to settle in that old Ute hunting ground halfway down."

Gerald frowns. "I know you and the others have the right to do as you wish, but Stands Alone and his band still hunt there."

Bent shrugs. Gerald and Suzanna exchange a glance, then she looks at the settlers. "You will be working on shares?"

The woman's husband nods. "Sí, señora. On land assigned to us." He glances at Bent. "On terms most generous."

She turns to Bent. "Of course, there will be other arrangements for those of us who were here before the grant was established."

Amusement glimmers in his face. He looks at Ramón, who's still standing behind her chair. Ramón spreads his hands as if in apology but doesn't smile.

Gerald looks around the room, at the watching settlers. "We'll discuss it later," he says. He and Bent nod to each other, but Suzanna frowns. After the visitors retreat down the hill to set up camp for the night, she follows Ramón into the kitchen, where he and Alma are working on dinner. "I don't like this," she says as she eases herself into a seat at the table.

"How are you feeling?" Alma asks.

Her mother scowls. "Tired. And worried." She turns to Ramón. "We need something in writing. Something that gives us more rights than those poor tenant farmers."

Alma's father and brother enter the kitchen from the outer door, their arms full of firewood. They add the split logs to the stack by the cast iron cookstove. "I'm not sure how long they'll be on the Poñil or anywhere else east of us," Gerald says. He crosses to the table and sits beside Suzanna. "Bent and Saint Vrain are escorting them to the Poñil, but they're not staying to help them set up. They're heading to Missouri."

"To buy trade goods?"

He shrugs. "That's what they're telling the settlers, but they told me privately that they've heard that the U.S. Army is mobilizing to push west. The American Congress has declared war on Mexico."

Ramón turns from the stove and Alma from the sink. "War?" she asks as he says, "¿Guerra?"

There's a long pause, then Ramón shakes his head, his kind face sober. "It has come at last."

"Yes. I expected it, and yet—"

The other man nods and turns back to the stove. Alma begins slicing summer squash into neat rounds.

Suzanna puts her face in her hands. "Invasion," she murmurs. "Those poor settlers."

"Won't the governor defend them?" Andrew asks from the door, where he's leaning against the wall.

Suzanna and Ramón humph at the same time. "Manuel Armijo?" she says derisively.

Ramón and Gerald exchange a grin. "Cuando el dinero habla, todos callan," Ramón says.

"When money talks, everyone shuts up?" Andrew asks.

Gerald chuckles. "It's a true saying, especially for someone like the governor." Then he sobers. He turns to Suzanna. "Bent says everything is likely to change once the U.S. takes over, so there's no point in putting any kind of agreement about the land on paper just yet. It would all have to be redone in proper American legal form after the army arrives. We might as well wait until there's a lawyer available to do it correctly."

Suzanna scowls. "If we do it before they arrive, the documents can include my name. But the Americans don't allow married women to own land. Which means I'll have nothing to pass on to Alma when I go."

"You aren't going anytime soon," Gerald says.

"Neither of has a will."

"There's no reason to worry about that for a good long while yet."

She gives him an exasperated, tight-lipped look and pushes back from the table. "I'm going to go lie down."

Suzanna's lips are still compressed the next morning when Saint Vrain and Charles Bent visit the cabin to say goodbye. She offers them coffee, trying to draw them inside for more conversation, but they remain on the porch.

"You truly do have a lovely location here," Saint Vrain says as he studies the mountains on the opposite side of the valley. Their tops are blushed pink by the light of the sun rising behind the cabin.

"Yes," Suzanna says. "It was nice when Ramón and Gerald chose it almost twenty years ago, and it's still delightful."

Gerald's lips twitch. She's been ambivalent about life in the valley for many years, so this statement is slightly out of character.

Suzanna turns to Charles Bent. "I'd like to make sure it remains in the family." Her hand presses her side.

"We'll need to negotiate a good price."

Her hand drops and her spine straightens. "We've been here eighteen years and done nothing but improve this land," she says. "Your entire grant is made more valuable by what we have shown can be done with it!"

He grins at her. "You're as bad as Padre Martínez. You never could take a joke."

She scowls. Her hand returns to her side. "And you never have known when to mitigate your tone and your greed."

Gerald's head tilts. "Suzanna—"

She shakes her head and moves into the house, hand still pressed to her side. Alma follows her.

On the porch, Ramón says, "The illness makes her speak without thinking."

In the cabin, Suzanna stops and half turns, eyes black with fury. Then her shoulders slump and she continues on toward the bedroom. "He's right, of course," she murmurs. "That was foolish of me."

Behind them, Saint Vrain's voice rumbles, lifting at the end, and the men all laugh companionably.

Suzanna smiles faintly. "Ceran's a hopeless flirt, but he has a good heart." Then her face darkens. "Which is more than I can say for Señor Charles Bent." As she moves into the cabin extension, past the big loom she hasn't touched in two years, she shakes her head. "I never have understood what your father sees in that man."

When Alma returns to the porch, the men are still there. Ceran Saint Vrain smiles at her as she closes the door behind her. "I failed to tell you yesterday that my goddaughter was married last week," he says. He glances at Charles Bent.

She brightens. "Rumalda? Who did she marry?"

"Thomas Boggs," Charles Bent says smugly. He looks at Gerald. "Governor Lilburn Boggs' oldest son."

Gerald nods, his square face impassive. The former Missouri governor does not impress him, though he likes Thomas well enough. He glances at Alma. "She's younger than you, isn't she?"

Alma nods. "About three years." She looks at Charles Bent. "Didn't she turn fifteen in February?"

Bent nods, and Alma's father raises an eyebrow, but Ceran Saint Vrain grins at him. "How old was Suzanna when you married?"

Gerald chuckles. "That was different."

Alma suppresses a smile. Her mother has often expressed a desire that her own daughter not rush into marriage, has said she herself was too young. Not for marriage, but for moving from Taos to the valley. For taking on the responsibilities and work the mountain farm entailed. For being so isolated.

Alma sobers. She hasn't seen Rumalda or any of her other Taos friends since the summer of 1842, four years ago. Before Grandfather Locke died. She sighs. "Everything changes," she says quietly.

The men are chatting and appear not to notice her comment. "Have you heard about Padre Martínez's latest excuse for causing trouble?" Charles Bent asks her father.

When Gerald shakes his head, he goes on. "A bunch of his family's cattle were run off by Ute Indians early this year. He got it into his head that I told them to do it." Bent makes a dismissive gesture. "In retaliation for his fighting the land grant, I suppose. But you know the calf. He talks a good deal, but his meaning disappears in all the noise."

Gerald raises an eyebrow. "The calf?"

"He sounds like one," Bent says defensively. "Always bawling about something."

"He remains el padre," Ramón says mildly. "It is a position which requires our respect."

"Not from me, it doesn't!" Bent's thin lips are tight with irritation. "He certainly hasn't earned it! Labeling my children bastards! Calling me a thief because I want to do something with land that's been sitting idle time out of mind! Accusing me of colluding with those damn Utes! It's his own people who were egging them on and buying those cows, not me!"

Alma is only half listening. She's still thinking about all the changes in her life. The adults seem to be wholly absorbed in Bent's diatribe about Padre Martínez, so she's surprised when, after Bent winds down and he and Saint Vrain head toward the waiting train of settlers, Ramón touches her shoulder. "Nothing lasts forever," he says gently.

She grins. "The feud between Padre Martínez and Charles Bent certainly seems like it will," she says.

He laughs. "That may be!"

CHAPTER 4 – MID-SEPTEMBER 1846
Moreno Valley, New Mexico

Alma wakes to the sound of sheep. Her mother had been restless in the night so the girl stayed beside her and now her own eyes and limbs are heavy with exhaustion. But the bawling of animals and barking of dogs is unmistakable. She glances at her mother. There's an unhappy crease in her forehead, but Suzanna's eyes are closed and her breathing is steady.

Alma creeps out of the room to the window in the weaving room.

Beyond the hay meadow in the valley below, a large herd of long-haired double-horned sheep moves south, heading out of the high pastures north of the cabin toward the pass to Taos. Two of the shepherds have stopped to talk with her father, who stands between the sheep and the fields. One of the men gestures south, then spreads his hands wide, palms up as if in surrender.

Ramón enters the room from the main cabin, carrying a tray that holds a cup of broth and a slice of soft wheat bread with no crust. He stops when he sees Alma at the window. "Tu madre, she sleeps?" he asks.

Alma nods and he moves to stand beside her and peer out the window. "The sheep return early from the high pastures," he says, frowning. "It is not a good sign."

She glances at him questioningly.

"It may be that the snows have already begun in the north," he explains. Then he shakes his head. "Or perhaps los hombres have received news which sends them home early."

"News of the Americans?"

He nods, watching the men below. Then a thin voice calls from the room behind them and they both turn.

"Here I am, Mama," Alma says as she enters the bedroom. "And Ramón has brought you some nice broth."

Suzanna's face twists as she struggles to sit up. "I hope I can do it justice." She looks up at the old man. "It seems such a waste to prepare food for me these days."

"You must take it, mi hija," he says gently. "It will strengthen you."

She gestures to Alma, who hurries to straighten the pillows. "I doubt I'll ever be truly strong again," Suzanna says. "But it is kind of you to say so."

Ramon has returned to his tasks and Suzanna has nibbled the bread, drunk a third of the broth, and settled back against the pillows when Gerald enters the room. He frowns at the food. "You should eat all of that," he scolds. But his heart isn't in it. When Suzanna waves a disparaging hand at him, he reaches for it, sinks into the chair beside the bed, and gently kisses her palm.

Alma leans to take the tray of half-eaten food, intending to leave them alone, but he turns his head toward her. "Could you ask Ramón to come in here?" he asks. "And your brother? The herders brought news which we all need to hear."

When everyone is gathered in the little room, Alma sitting on the foot of the bed, Ramón standing beside her, and Andrew leaning against the wall by the door, her father says, "There's news from Santa Fe."

"Los americanos have arrived?" Ramón asks.

Gerald nods.

Andrew shifts his weight. "Was there a battle?"

"No." Gerald grins at Suzanna. "You were right. Governor Armijo didn't fight. In fact, he seems to have literally run away, leaving someone else to officially surrender New Mexico to the U.S. Army."

"He ran away?"

"He took some of the cannon and about a hundred men and headed toward Chihuahua." He shrugs. "At least, that's what the shepherds said they were told. The story is third hand at best, so it may not be true in all its details."

"But the Americans have taken over," Ramón says.

Gerald nods. "Yes. Also, there's a rumor that Charles Bent will be named Governor and Carlos Beaubien will be one of three judges. And Luis Lee will be appointed sheriff at Taos."

Suzanna frowns. "Are all the authorities going to be anglos?"

He shrugs. "As I said, it's a rumor."

Ramón's face is grave. "It does not bode well."

Andrew pushes away from the wall. "We should go and find out what's happening for ourselves."

The others swing toward him. "There's hay to be brought in," his father says.

"And corn to be gathered," Ramón adds.

Alma rises from the bed. "Mama is too weak to go anywhere just yet." She turns to smile at her mother. "You need to eat and grow stronger so we can satisfy Andrew's curiosity."

They all chuckle at this, even the boy as he runs a hand through his curls. "I'll work harder on the hay if you'll eat," he tells his mother. She smiles at him but then her eyes close and her head sinks gratefully into her pillows as the others follow him out of the room.

TERESINA

CHAPTER 5 – OCTOBER 1846
Taos, New Mexico

My father was a thin-skinned man, quick to judgement and slow to forgive. We children learned early how to please him with eager words and sweet looks. I suspect he felt constricted by what he saw as willfulness. Others', as well as his own. My mother's Catholicism, his own inability to bow to any man. Especially Padre Martínez, a priest as stubborn and quick to anger as himself.

Father craved land and the security it brought—the status and titles. Calling him "Don Carlos" pleased him greatly. Did this desire for recognition from others stem from his friendship with Charles Beaubien? Never feeling as if he quite equaled the other man?

Not that the Frenchmen spoke of his noble ancestry. His women did that for him. But it must have rankled in my father, who was fiercely proud of what he and his brothers had made of themselves: the trading fort on the Arkansas River, the stores in Taos and Santa Fe.

Yet he was drawn to Carlos Beaubien, in spite of their differences. Father could barely spell English. Beaubien, edu-

cated for the priesthood, was articulate in three languages as well as Latin. Yet the French-Canadian man valued father's business acumen, his sharp wit. And his knowledge of the empty lands east and north of Taos, where land grants might be available.

But Father always seemed to crave still more status. When the news of his appointment as governor arrived, his pale face flushed with pleasure, his eyes lit up. And then he immediately sobered, tried to look stern and burdened with the weight of his new office. But he stood straighter, somehow.

My mother was not happy about the new position. Her forehead grooved with worry as she shook her head and asked if Father was certain he wished to accept the post. There would be trouble. She was sure of it. The position would be full of difficulties.

He waved her concerns away. "Even that big-mouthed padre will have to listen to me now," he said, his eyes glittering.

She studied him for a long moment and turned away. "I fear it will not end well," she murmured to Rumalda, who was seated next to the fire combing out Estefina's hair.

The problems Mother foresaw began almost at once. As my father gathered his things to make the trip to Santa Fe and take up his new position, someone pounded on the courtyard gate. Alfredo went to answer it and returned with a tall slim Taos Pueblo man.

"Ah, Tomás Romero!" my father said. "You have heard the news?"

"Buenas noches, Don Carlos," the other man said. "May I congratulate you on your new position?"

Father's lips curved disparagingly, though his eyes were bright with pleasure. "It may not be worthy of congratulations, but I thank you." He gestured toward the end of the room and the small space beyond, which he used as a kind of office for meeting with people and for storing his shotgun and pistols. "How may I help you?"

"It is about the fences," Señor Romero said as they moved toward the other room. "As you are aware, the cattle intrude on the pueblo fields—"

Father stopped in the doorway and held up his hand, palm facing the Taos leader. "Fences are not in my purview," he said. "You'll have to go to Cornelio Vigil for that. He is the prefect here."

"But you as governor—"

"We are no longer under Mexican rule, with governors who do whatever they damn well please and ride roughshod over local decisions," Father said. "Under American law, local leaders have jurisdiction over things such as fences. Take your petition to Don Cornelio."

Señor Romero studied him for a long minute. There was something between sorrow and disgust in his face, but Father didn't see it. He was moving back into the larger room and gesturing to Mother's long-time servant, Guadalupe. "Chocolate," he told her.

Tomás Romero shook his head. "I beg your indulgence, señor," he said formally. "But I must return to my people and discuss how best to resolve this issue ourselves."

"Speak to Don Cornelio," Father said impatiently.

"I fear it will be of little use. El prefect is closely related to one of the persons who owns the cattle in question."

"Then take them to court."

"It is not our way."

Father's voice had a triumphant edge now. "You'd best learn to accommodate yourselves to the new ways, then. The old ones will be of little use to you now."

The other man nodded, his face a careful mask. "I fear you speak truly. I bid you good day."

Father gestured to Alfredo to see Romero out as my mother watched them all with anxious eyes.

ALMA

CHAPTER 6 – OCTOBER 1846
Moreno Valley, New Mexico

The hills that line the long mountain valley are blazing with gold when Suzanna takes to her bed for the last time. She has fussed at Gerald about getting the late hay in, asked Ramón to gather fresh willow bark from the lowest of the beaver ponds in Cimarron Canyon, and told Andrew to open the bedroom window to let in the October air.

He now hovers in the doorway as Alma arranges her mother's pillows, tucks the yellow-and-green wool shawl around her shoulders, and smooths the covers over her legs.

Suzanna touches the reddish-brown stripes in the top blanket. "This is the one you wove."

Alma grins as she settles into the chair beside the bed. "Not very well. We'll set up a new one as soon as you're able, so you can help me with my technique." She nods to the shawl. "I'd also like to make a duplicate of that for myself."

Suzanna closes her eyes, then opens them again, looking at Alma, then Andrew. "You'll have to do it on your own."

"You'll recover," Andrew says, his voice deeper than usual.

"You always have," Alma agrees.

Suzanna shakes her head. "Not this time." She touches her abdomen. "It's worse now."

"Can't you—?" Andrew breaks off.

"I'm sorry." She takes Alma's hand in hers as she stretches the other toward Andrew. He moves across the room, kneels beside the bed, and takes it.

"I had hoped—" She closes her eyes, then starts again. "You are such good children. I have been so blessed by you."

He makes a choking sound. "Mama—"

She smiles at him and releases his hand. "Go," she says. "See if there are any butterflies left in the marsh."

He stands, bends to kiss her forehead, and heads for the door without speaking. The floorboards shudder in the outer room as he passes the loom.

Chaser IV comes in and shuffles into the place Andrew left behind. He lays his big head on the blankets. "Good dog," Suzanna murmurs. She pats him feebly and smiles at Alma. "Our first Chaser saved my life. Now this one sees me out."

"Oh, don't—"

She raises a thin hand. "Tell your father to bury me in Taos," she whispers. "If he can." She stops, waits for her breath to return, then adds, "If my carcass won't decompose too much before he can get it there." She frowns. Her voice is reedy, but still fierce. More of a hiss than a command, but still adamant. "And tell him to get those damn papers for the land before he comes back to the valley."

Alma pats her hand. "You will go with him and see to it yourself, just as soon you're able."

Suzanna moves impatiently. "Promise me."

Alma nods, tears welling into her eyes. "I didn't know you were so ill," she whispers. Her throat hurts. She can barely speak.

"I did my best to hide it. To protect you all."

"I wish I had known."

Her mother smiles and turns her head. She pats the dog. "It's what mothers do," she whispers. "You will make sacrifices for your own children someday." She closes her eyes again. "I had hoped to see that for myself." Tears slip from her eyes, and she dabs at them ineffectually. "Foolish," she murmurs.

Chaser lifts his head, stretches to snuff at her face, then pads out of the room. "Stay with me," Suzanna whispers and Alma nods, unable to speak. She tightens her grip on her mother's fingers.

They stay as they are through the long morning, until Suzanna's breathing finally stops.

Alma has dozed off. She wakes to find the cabin an empty shell, the sunlight too bright, the air from the open window biting cold. She slips her fingers from her mother's limp hand and moves out of the room, past the silent loom and on to the main living area.

She stands there for a long time, listening to the silent house. This is what it will be like now. No mother opinions, no calling for the dog, no thump of the loom. No—

Alma swallows the pain in her throat and moves to the porch. Her father is cutting hay in the meadow below, moving across the field as if scything the long grass is all that remains between him and sanity. Alma knows what he's doing, because she's done it herself these past weeks, keeping grief at bay with stolid activity.

But not today. Today she's wrung out, her knees quivering at the thought of the path before her. She takes a deep breath and moves down the hill.

Andrew is on his stomach at the edge of the field, the dog beside him. The boy's curly head is focused on a thin line of ants which move steadily between the mown hay and their nest mound, storing grass seed.

The mastiff is asleep, drowsing in the sunlight. He wakes when Andrew spies Alma and moves into a sitting position. They both look at her questioningly but tears well in her eyes and she has to turn away. Andrew puts a hand to his face.

Alma moves toward the field. Her father has his back to her. "Papa," she says.

He doesn't turn. Perhaps he hasn't heard her. Perhaps he doesn't want to.

"Papa!" she calls.

He turns, his square face bleak and questioning. She nods and he drops the scythe and comes toward her. "I'm sorry I left it to you."

She pushes her curls from her face, tears suddenly prickling. "It's all right. She told me—" Alma stops, takes a breath. "She wants to be buried in Taos."

"Wanted," Andrew says. He's standing behind her, hands in his pockets. His face twists and he looks away. "Wanted. Past tense."

She feels the tears again and turns to her father, who's staring blindly at the cows grazing in the pasture south of the meadow.

"That is, if you think the body won't decompose too much on the way."

His lips quirk. "She said that?"

Alma nods.

He squints at the cows again, then at the mountains at the southern end of the valley, hazy in the distance. "Where's Ramón?"

"She asked him to go down the canyon this morning to get some fresh willow bark from the growth by the lower beaver pond."

His head swings toward her. "She specified the location?"

"Yes."

"The one farthest from the house. That was kind of her." He turns slowly, looking at the western peaks, the golden aspens on their flanks, the intense blue of the sky above. Behind him, in the wetlands where the Cimarron River begins, a black bird sings raucously.

"I'd hoped to bury her on the hillside behind the cabin," he says. "Beside my father." Then he sighs. "But this valley never did feel like home to her. And having her in Taos will comfort your Grandfather Peabody."

He turns north, looking up at Old Baldy, its top mantled with snow. "Let's see what Ramón thinks. If we can get her to Taos, we will." He glances at Alma and she nods, noting the exhaustion in his gray eyes. First his father, and now his wife, who had never loved this valley but had made a home here because she loved him.

Alma shivers a little. Something moves on the path at the edge of the wetlands. Ramón. And someone beside him, in full Ute regalia.

"It's Stands Alone," Andrew says, peering past her. "Looks like he has his whole family with him."

* * * *

She has left us," the Ute man says.

Alma's father nods. "You felt it too."

Stands Alone's eyes glimmer with amusement. "Ramón, he told me."

Ramón raises his head. "She was mi ahijada, my goddaughter. I felt it."

Alma's hand twitches, reaching toward him, but she restrains herself. If she touches him now, her own barrier will break and there will be no end to the weeping.

She turns away, and finds Stands Alone's oldest wife, Sings Quietly, beside her.

"Por favor," the woman says. "I see her?" When Alma nods, she takes the girl's arm and they move toward the cabin. Chirping Bird, the younger wife, follows.

When they reach the room, the two Ute women stand respectfully, studying the figure on the bed, then turn to Alma. "Agua," Chirping Bird says gently. "Por favor."

"We will care for her," Sings Quietly tells Alma. "You must rest now."

Alma stares at the two women, wondering how they know how much she has been dreading the necessary steps to prepare her mother's body. Sings Quietly smiles at her sadly. "Go now," she says. "Bring water."

Alma's eyes sting with gratitude as she turns to the door.

After she's delivered the water, Alma moves to the porch, where the men find her an hour later. As Alma's father explains to Ramón and Stands Alone that Suzanna wanted to be buried in Taos, the two Ute women appear. They stop, staring at him, then Ramón stirs.

"It should be as she wished," he says. He looks at the women. "The body, it will arrive smelling sweet?"

Sings Quietly purses her lips. "Not evil."

He turns to Alma's father. "It would please Don Jeremiah."

Gerald nods. "Yes."

There's another long silence, then Stands Alone says, "You all go. We will stay to guard cattle." He turns to Alma's father. "The American soldiers have taken our grazing lands. We winter in the mountains this year."

Gerald studies him, then nods. "I would be grateful," he says.

But by the time the buckboard wagon is packed and ready the next day, Ramón has elected to stay behind. "I cannot see her buried," he says, his face twisting. "I cannot see the pain of her father." He turns to Alma. "Forgive me, nita. I cannot."

She studies his face, suddenly noticing how wrinkled it is, the new threads of white in his black hair, the deep sorrow in his eyes.

He sees her anxiety and smiles sadly. "The valley will heal me."

Chaser IV has come to stand beside him. The dog whines and nudges his hand, then hers. "His presence will also help," Ramón says, smiling slightly.

Alma bends to stroke the dog's big head, then gives Ramón a tight hug and climbs onto the wagon seat beside her brother. Her father flicks the reins at the mules, and they move across the yard past the barn and down the slope onto the track to Taos. Alma huddles into her mother's green-and-yellow shawl and stares blindly into the middle distance.

Ramón is so sure the valley can heal. But she feels nothing. There's only a numbness, a hollow space between her ribs, a heaviness in her head. Not even the calls of the blackbirds in the marsh or the gold of the aspens on the lower mountain slopes can warm her heart.

CHAPTER 7 – NOVEMBER 1846
Taos Canyon, New Mexico

The weather turns cold as the Locke wagon works its way over Palo Flechado Pass and west down Taos Creek. Ice clings to the stream's banks. The buckboard bumps awkwardly over the frozen ruts in the old road. Alma shivers and tightens her mother's shawl around her shoulders. The gray weather matches her mood. It also fulfills her mother's wishes. Suzanna's body will be too cold to have decomposed much before they reach the village of Don Fernando de Taos where she was born and raised.

They enter the village in late morning on the third day. Incongruously, the sun comes out as her grandfather's house comes into sight. Alma closes her eyes against it. Her father shifts on the plank seat beside her. Her mother was ill for a long time, yet none of them realized how sick she actually was. Grandfather Peabody will be unprepared for their arrival.

Most of the walls along the street are six feet high, so no one sees the wagon go past. As it turns into the gate of the Peabody compound, Alma's grandfather comes from the stable area at the back, a shovel in one hand and wood pitchfork in the other. His gray chin beard is speckled with straw.

His blue eyes brighten when he sees them. He leans the tools next to the bench by the house door and brushes his beard with his fingers as he hurries forward.

"What a wonderful surprise!" he says. Then their somber faces and Suzanna's absence register. "What is it?" He looks past the children to Gerald. "Where is my daughter?"

Gerald gestures mutely at the carefully wrapped body in the wagon bed. The old man's narrow face crumples. "Why didn't you—"

"It was very sudden, abuelo," Alma says gently. Andrew clambers down from the wagon, then reaches up to help her, and she goes to her grandfather and wraps her arms around him. "We had no time to send word."

Gerald is down now and coming around the wagon to face his father-in-law. "She didn't tell me how bad it was," he says. He spreads his hands. "You know Suzanna. I would have sent for you if I'd known."

Jeremiah Peabody nods. "She was always so stubborn." The two men turn to gaze at the body. Jeremiah shudders, then straightens and puts a hand on Gerald's arm. "But you have brought her to me."

"She wanted to be buried in Taos," Andrew says.

Jeremiah frowns. "Did she say where? There is no cemetery here for Protestants."

Gerald looks at Alma, who shakes her head.

"I will consult with Bent—" her grandfather begins, then stops. "But he is in Santa Fe, of course, not here. I keep forgetting." He turns to Gerald. "He's been named Governor."

Gerald raises an eyebrow. "Have he and Saint Vrain come back from Missouri?"

"Charles has returned. Saint Vrain apparently stayed behind to bring the merchant goods in the annual train." He turns to consider Suzanna's body. "Carlos Beaubien might have some ideas. Or we can ask Luis Lee. He's the sheriff here now and should know of a plot of land we can buy."

Alma frowns. "Benigna Lee's father?" She remembers him as a vacillating man, quite tall, but not very forceful. Not someone who would really be comfortable as sheriff. Although he did have a sharp tongue and was quite concerned about the property rights of foreign-born residents like himself.

"Yes." Her grandfather says. He turns to Gerald. "You know he joined forces with the Beaubiens a few years ago to request a land grant north of the Red River."

Gerald frowns. "Carlos has a grant in addition to the one that includes the valley?"

"No, this was Lee and Narciso, the Beaubien son."

Andrew moves impatiently toward the end of the wagon and begins lowering the tailgate.

"We should get her inside," Alma says.

The two men turn and look at her blankly, then her grandfather reaches for the side of the wagon. "I—"

"It doesn't seem real to me, either," she says gently.

Gerald pats the older man's shoulder as he moves past to help Andrew lift the thin corpse from its bed. Jeremiah Peabody passes his hand over his face, steadies himself, then nods toward the house. "We'll put her in her old room."

When they enter the hall, a short plump woman with black hair coiled in a crown around her head is standing in the kitchen doorway, looking impatient and skeptical at the same time. Her eyes are mere slits above her high cheekbones.

"Anamaria, this is my son-in-law Gerald Locke and also my grandchildren, Alma and Andrew," Jeremiah says. He turns to the others. "This is Anamaria Pacheco, my new housekeeper."

"Buenos días," she says formally. Her gaze drifts to the body in Gerald's arms.

"My daughter has—" Jeremiah's voice chokes off as the woman's face changes.

"¡Dios mío!" She looks at Gerald, then the children. "What a terrible thing." She turns to Jeremiah and flaps her hands. "You go now. Find the priest. I will arrange everything here." She moves down the hall, taking charge, waving Gerald after her. "Come bring her into the cold room and I will prepare her."

Alma follows tentatively, watching the housekeeper, who moves jugs and pots off a long adobe bench that runs along the end wall, and gestures for Gerald to place the body there. Gerald steps back and she orders him curtly to leave, then begins removing Suzanna's wraps.

"She has already been washed and dressed," Alma says, hoping to stop her. She doesn't want this stranger handling her mother's body.

Anamaria's hands drop to her sides. She straightens and turns to the girl with a sympathetic look. "You did it yourself?"

Alma shakes her head. "Two Ute women, friends of ours, helped me."

The other woman sniffs. "Utes? They wouldn't know what to do. Or the proper procedure." She turns back to the body and begins lifting layers of clothing and peering suspiciously at the skin underneath. As she smooths each section of fabric back into place, she murmurs a prayer in Spanish.

Alma's hands tighten. This has already been done. Sings Quietly and Chirping Bird also said prayers, though in their own language. It seems like sacrilege to allow this stranger to interfere, to somehow mitigate their kindness.

But then her grandfather is at the door. His grieving face softens when he sees what the housekeeper is doing, and Alma goes to him. If Anamaria's actions comfort him, then she will not intervene.

* * * *

Because Suzanna was a Protestant, the usual village procession to the burial ground is not appropriate, but she is well accompanied through the streets to her resting place. Charles Bent's wife, Ignacia, takes the lead, her five-year-old daughter Teresina hiding behind her skirts. Ignacia's sister Josefa walks beside them. Her large brown eyes are tender with concern, which makes her seem younger than her eighteen years.

Sheriff Lee's daughter Benigna and Ignacia's fifteen-year-old Rumalda are just behind them, flanking a regal Luz Beaubien. They walk ahead of the coffin, while Alma and her brother follow with their father and grandfather.

Sheriff Lee, Thomas Boggs, Benigna's husband José Pley, and Ignacia and Josefa's brother Pablo Jaramillo carry the coffin, one man at each corner. Anamaria has remained at the house, preparing the meal that will follow.

Alma knows she should be grateful to these people for coming to support her family in their sorrow, but she feels strangely disconnected from them all. The bustle of preparations, the need to comfort her grandfather, have kept her emotions at bay these past two days. But now it's almost over. There has been an odd comfort in having her mother's body nearby. A strange half hope that it was all a bad dream. That Suzanna would stir, push back her coverings, and demand to know why no one was tending the corn or harvesting hay.

Tears well in Alma's eyes. She turns to her father, but he's staring straight ahead, at a pain uniquely his own. Andrew walks on his other side, his face averted.

And her grandfather— He seems stunned. Bowed down. As she watches, he looks up at the sky and blinks rapidly. He tilts slightly toward her, as if the ground is uneven under his feet. Alma reaches for his hand.

And then they are in the field where her mother is to be buried. It's a sizable piece of land, with trees along the irrigation channel at the far end, where the little wooden gates to the field have long been closed off. Padre Martínez's housekeeper owns it. She's sent word through Rumalda that Señor Peabody is welcome to bury his only daughter there.

A space has been cleared for the coffin at the near end of the field. The little procession pauses beside the hole, not quite knowing how to proceed. Pablo Jaramillo half turns toward Gerald and his father-in-law. "It is customary—" he begins.

But then Rumalda speaks up. "Here is el padre," she says, gesturing toward the other end of the field.

Padre Martínez emerges from the path along the irrigation ditch and heads toward them. As he gets closer, he makes the sign of the cross, as if blessing them all, then stops in front of Jeremiah Peabody. "I am forbidden to give her the full rites of the church," he says apologetically.

Jeremiah nods.

"However, with your permission, I would be honored to say a few words and provide a simple prayer."

Jeremiah glances at Gerald, who nods. Andrew lifts his head. "She wouldn't like it."

Gerald shrugs, his eyes dull. "There's no harm in it."

Andrew frowns, but Alma gives him a warning look. The priest believes he's doing them a kindness, and the others will expect words to be spoken. And it may comfort Grandfather Peabody. Andrew nods reluctantly. Padre Martínez steps forward.

When it is over and the coffin is covered with soil, they all make their way back to the house and Alma busies herself with helping Anamaria serve the guests. Finally, the casa is empty, and she can slip away to the little adobe-walled cubicle that was once her mother's and wrap the green-and-yellow shawl around her shoulders as she weeps.

CHAPTER 8 – EARLY DECEMBER 1846
Taos, New Mexico

"I'm glad you decided to stay in Don Fernando de Taos for the holidays," Alma's grandfather says. He moves the food on his plate around aimlessly as he smiles at Alma and her brother. "It is good to see you again at my table." His face softens a little as he looks at Andrew. "And to share my books with you."

Andrew smiles back at him. "The natural history ones, at any rate."

Alma closes her eyes. The books had been her mother's. Someone touches Alma's forearm. Her father's brown fingers. She turns toward him, but he averts his gaze and returns to his food, his face tired and sad. She has a sudden urge to fling herself into his arms, force him to weep the tears she herself has not shed since the day her mother was buried.

But her grandfather is speaking, his eyes on her father's square face. "I hope you are not in a hurry to return. In fact, I'm not sure you would be able to do so if you tried. I'm told that the snowfall in the mountains this year is heavier than usual. I doubt you could get the buckboard over the pass."

Her father nods without looking up from his plate. "I'm in no hurry." He glances at Alma. "And I need to talk to Carlos Beaubien about the land grant."

"You haven't yet attended to that?" her grandfather asks.

Gerald shakes his head and helps himself to another tortilla. "He hasn't been in town much these last few months. He nor Bent."

A smile flickers on her grandfather's lips. "Yes, Padre Martínez commented just yesterday that they seemed very busy in Santa Fe with their new toy government."

"I wish they would come back, so you can get it settled, Papa," Andrew says. "I want to go home."

A shadow crosses Gerald's face. "I'm sorry, son. I'm not ready yet."

Something in Alma's chest loosens. She's not ready to return, either. There are plenty of reminders of her mother here: her books, her childhood bed. But they aren't as sharply defined by her absence as the cabin's contents will be. There, every board, every strand of woven fiber, every glimpse of the valley through the glass windows she fought so hard for, will remind Alma of her loss. She isn't sure she ever wants to go back.

"I'm also told the Saint Vrain train has arrived in Santa Fe," her grandfather says. He glances at Andrew. "Beaubien's son has apparently finished his schooling at the college outside St. Louis and accompanied the wagons from Missouri."

Andrew brightens. "Narciso?" He looks at his father. "I suppose staying a little longer would be all right. He'll be sure to be home for the Christmas celebrations."

As his father and grandfather smile sadly at him, Anamaria comes in. "Pardon, señores," she says. "Señor Tomás Romero is here to see you."

Gerald glances at his father-in-law, but she says, "He requested to speak with both of you, señores."

Jeremiah pushes back from the table as Gerald shrugs and gets up.

"May I come, too?" Alma asks. Her grandfather nods and Andrew reaches for another tortilla as the three of them leave the room.

The Taos pueblo leader has come to discuss the Beaubien Miranda land grant. "Concern has increased among my people that our hunting grounds will be restricted and our sacred lake there on the mountain will be polluted by the presence of strangers," he explains.

Gerald lifts an eyebrow. "Do you think anyone will really venture that far up? Surely no one will want to farm or even graze their herds there, when there's so much land below."

Romero shakes his head. "Now that los americanos have come, there is talk of searching for the rocks precious to them."

"Rocks precious—" Gerald frowns. "You mean gold and silver?"

Romero nods. "Our men have met soldiers in the mountains, on leave from Santa Fe. They had steel axes with sharp points." He moves his hand, demonstrating the length of the axe blade, the way it ends in a sharp 'v'. "Also large metal pans," he says. "Very shallow, for washing—" He pauses. "Is it correct, this term? For moving el agua about."

"Pickaxes," Alma's grandfather says. "And the necessary equipment for washing gold at a placer mine site."

"I'll be damned," her father says.

"This is why I come to you," Romero says. "They will reach your valley by planting time."

"If they haven't already." Gerald says. He looks at Alma. "They'll be tearing up the hillsides, if they think there's something there."

Anamaria comes in, carrying a tray of coffee cups and biscochitos. Alma rises to help her distribute the food and drink. "But they won't find anything, will they?" she asks. She moves toward Tomás Romero with a cup of coffee, but the housekeeper is ahead of her, dipping her head to the tall man solicitously.

He smiles at her, then looks at Alma gravely. "They may find what they seek. Our warriors have sometimes brought their women strange lumps of brown rock which does not break and can be shined to a pleasant glow. We beat them with hammers and create pendants and other ornamentation."

Gerald frowns. "Copper?"

"It certainly sounds like it," Jeremiah says.

Tomás Romero puts his cup down and turns to Gerald. "You have lived in that valley many winters."

Gerald nods. "Nineteen, come this spring."

"And my people have hunted there since the beginning of time. We must protect it from los americanos."

"Governor Armijo gave it to Carlos Beaubien and Guadalupe Miranda before the American Army arrived."

"Sí. That was not a good thing. Padre Martínez advocated for us." He nods toward Gerald's father-in-law. "Also Don Jeremiah. Even their voices could not persuade el gobernador." He shakes his head. "And now Bent is in his place. He is part owner of the granted land." He looks at Gerald, then Jeremiah. "You know this?"

When they nod, he makes a disgusted sound with his lips. "There is now no peaceful means to stop the theft of our land and its use for evil."

"Evil?" Alma asks.

He turns toward her, eyes dark in his strong face. "Cutting into the land to remove what is hidden is a desecration. To do so destroys the sacred balance which keeps us all whole."

Her father lifts a skeptical eyebrow, but Alma leans toward the Taos leader. "The sacred balance?"

He studies her, his face softening. "You have felt it, I think. The soil and grasses speak to you."

She sits back. How does he know this? Then, compelled by his gaze, she nods.

"But I break the soil when I plow," her father says. "As your people do when you plant your corn."

"Sí. Before we plant, we prepare special ceremonies and invoke the saint of the Spanish, San Ysidro. We ask him to allow the plants to grow and feed us." His lips twist. "We open the earth with reverence and for food, not shiny rocks."

"Yet you take the rocks you find there to your women. You turn them into objects of beauty."

"They have been left for us on the surface of the earth. We do not hunt them or destroy the soil to uncover them."

Alma frowns, confused. "I have heard of a place south of the city of Santa Fe," she says tentatively. "In the mountains east of the pueblo of Santo Domingo, where the people dig in the caves for pieces of turquoise."

He nods. "Sí, the sacred blue stone of the sky. It is said that the first peoples found pieces lying on the bare mountainside, waiting to be discovered. Now some dig to find more. I do not agree that they should do this thing, but I know it is done."

"And those people are from the pueblo of Santo Domingo, not Taos," her grandfather says drily.

The two men share a bemused look, the interaction of old friends with many hours of conversation between them.

"And now you wish to protect the hillsides of my valley," Alma's father says.

"Also of our sacred lake and all that lies between and around them."

"How would you suggest we do that?"

"I am told you have not yet sought permission from these new owners—" His mouth twists slightly, then he goes on, re-phrasing the statement. "That Beaubien and the others may not allow you to remain unmolested where you have placed yourself."

Gerald nods. "Because of his new duties, I have been unable to speak with Carlos Beaubien. He is not often in town."

The Taos leader nods. "It is so. And you are grieving the loss of your woman."

"Yes." There's a long silence, then Romero stands. "I will leave you now, to think of what has been spoken here."

The men say their goodbyes and Alma silently accompanies the Taos man to the outer door, then across the courtyard to the gate. He pauses there and looks down at her. "You are a woman of great strength, drawn from the soil of your valley," he says quietly. "Do not stay too long from your land."

And then he is gone, Alma staring after him. Clouds drift overhead. The sky is a brilliant blue. Something in her heart shifts. The pain of her loss is unbearable. Perhaps home is the answer.

TERESINA

CHAPTER 9 - DECEMBER 12-13, 1846
Taos, New Mexico

I have seldom seen my mother so angry. She had knelt quietly during the special Saturday mass to celebrate Our Lady of Guadalupe, her head bowed devoutly as Padre Martínez spoke the words of the annual liturgy in the Virgin's honor. And she had lingered politely afterwards, exchanging greetings with the women around us.

In fact, Mother was so polite that by the time we moved from the church into the bright December morning, the priest had already changed his vestments and was mingling with the other parishioners. As we approached him, he patted the arm of the man he was talking to and said jovially, "Get your weapons ready! You might need them!" Then he saw my mother and grinned. "Or learn to speak inglés!"

My mother frowned and the man with him looked at her guiltily, muttered, "Buenos días," and slipped away.

But el padre only laughed at Mama's expression, his high forehead shining in the sun. "A joke, Ignacia!" he said. "It was a joke!"

Her frown deepened. "You tell them to fight los americanos?"

"¡Fue una broma!" he said again. "It was a joke!"

Her eyes sharpened. "It was talk of insurrection. We are part of los Estados Unidos de América now. We must accommodate ourselves."

The priest shrugged his big shoulders. "There are those who think differently."

She glared at him, but he shook his head and smiled at her benignly. "Oh, Ignacia," he said. "Even as a girl you were unwilling to listen to anyone's opinion but your own. No wonder you chose to cohabitate with that heathen Charles Bent."

She pulled me closer to her. "You should speak more politely of mi esposo. He is el gobernador now."

Martínez's eyes narrowed. "And you should remember that he is not your husband in the eyes of holy church and that I am el padre, the priest, not one of your children or sisters." He glanced at me. "There may come a time when I refuse to baptize the offspring of women such as you and the heathen rabble you bind yourselves to."

She opened her mouth, then closed it and reached for my hand. "Come Teresina," she said, her eyes snapping at the priest. "Let us seek kinder and more enlightened conversation."

Then she stopped talking. She was tightlipped as she silently gathered up my sister and brother, and spoke to no one on the way home.

Alfredo did his best to engage her. "Señora Lee asked me if I had practiced sufficiently for Las Posadas," he said. This event was a reenactment of the experiences of Mary and Joseph the night before the Holy Child's birth, as they searched for a room in Bethlehem. On each evening of the nine days before Christmas, the entire village escorted small carved bultos, or statues, of the two saints through the village, seeking shelter for them. Alfredo had been asked to carry the San José, who father called Saint Joseph. It was considered a great honor.

Mother didn't respond to his comments.

When we entered the house, we found that Rumalda and Josefa had already returned and were helping to prepare the meal. Rumalda knelt by the hearth and Josefa was at the table mixing masa in a large brown mica-flecked pottery bowl.

Estefina crossed to the table and began measuring out the corn flour for her. Alfredo and I stayed by the door.

Mother had worn her largest rebozo that morning, against the cold. Now she began unwrapping it from her head and shoulders. Then she suddenly stopped, her eyes blazing. "He threatened not to baptize my future children!"

Everyone went still. "¿El padre?" Josefa asked.

Mama tore the rebozo off, flung it to one side, and began stalking up and down the room.

Josefa turned questioningly to Alfredo. When he looked away, she raised her eyebrows at me, and I nodded.

"I should refuse to allow Alfredo to participate in Las Posadas!" Mama fumed.

Alfredo stiffened. "But next year I'll be too old to carry the San José!"

Josefa shot him a warning look. We all knew it was wiser to allow Mama's steam to run out when she was angry. "We need more wood for the fire," Josefa told him.

Alfredo's shoulders slumped, but he turned to the door.

As soon as it closed behind him, Rumalda got up from the hearth. "Carrying the bulto of San José is a great honor," she said, pushing her long wavy hair from her forehead.

"He was invited to do it by the organizers, not el padre," *Josefa added.*

"And he is correct that he will be too old next year," *Rumalda said. "Tomás was surprised they even invited him to do it this season."*

"It was in acknowledgement of his father's new role," Mama said. "That, and to make sure the statue isn't dropped this time."

"I felt so badly for the little boy who dropped it on the third night last year," Josefa said. "He was so anxious all the evenings remaining."

My mother's lips twitched. "Poor pequeña," she said. She turned away. "And it will be too late now to find another child able to take on the role. I suppose Alfredo must go on with it." She sighed and bent to pick up her rebozo. She flipped it outward, letting it flutter into a straight line. It was an exceptionally beautiful one made of dark blue merino wool Father had brought from Missouri. "Here, Teresina, help me fold this."

As I crossed the room, Alfredo came in, his arms full of firewood, eyes anxious. Josefa and Rumalda smiled at him encouragingly and he turned to Mama and stood waiting.

"It's all right," she said begrudgingly. "I won't forbid it." She turned to Rumalda. "However, I will make a note in my memoranda book of what Padre Martínez said this morning. Mi esposo should know of his activities. They should be recorded."

We didn't go to mass the next day. My mother was still angry at the padre and besides, we'd attended the service for Our Lady of Guadalupe the day before. So we had a bit of a late start and were just finishing our midday meal when Sheriff Lee's daughter, Benigna, arrived for a visit.

After the usual greetings and inquiries into the health of various family members, including her husband, who was gone on a trapping expedition, my mother looked at Benigna expectantly. Although she, Rumalda, and Aunt Josefa were good friends and saw each other often, it was unusual for Benigna to pay a formal visit. And she seemed a little nervous.

She patted the blond curls carefully arranged on her shoulders, straightened in her seat, and turned to Mama. "I believe you know that my mother is one of the sponsors of Las Posadas this year," she began. She smiled at Alfredo. "She tells me you are well prepared to play your role this Wednesday evening and all the days after."

Mama nodded, although she didn't smile. "Yes, he has been practicing diligently and has learned to walk with great dignity and assurance."

"I'm sure he will do well." Benigna pleated her skirt between her fingers, then looked up. "Mi madre tells me a problem has arisen with the child who was to carry Our Lady."

Mother's eyes narrowed. "A problem?"

"The little girl is unwell." Benigna shook her head. "Las curanderas have been unable to heal her. The poor little one has been ailing all this fall. Mama and the others thought the honor of processing in Las Posadas might help her, but still she is ill. Her parents don't wish to expose her to the excitement of nine days of night air."

My mother nodded. "That is wise of them."

There was a long silence. Benigna pleated her skirt again. Rumalda leaned forward. "And so?"

Benigna looked at my mother from the corner of her eyes. "Mi madre and the others have asked me to request that your daughter take on the responsibility of carrying the figure of Our Lady."

Across the room, Estefina sat up straight, her eyes shining. Benigna shot her a glance and looked down at her skirt again, then at me.

Mother nodded. "I'm sure Estefina will be delighted—"

Benigna looked up. "They would like a younger child this year." She glanced at me. "The girl who carried Our Lady last year was considerably larger than the boy who carried that of San José, and many participants felt it was disrespectful."

Alfredo, who resented Estefina's recent growth spurt, smirked, and Estefina slumped back in her seat, scowling at me. My head buzzed with excitement.

My mother studied me with a concerned look. "Do you think you can do it, Teresina?"

I nodded, afraid to breathe.

"It is a great responsibility, Teresina," Benigna said gently. "A task that must be undertaken with dignity and respect."

I lifted my head. "I am not a little child. I am five years old. I can carry myself with great dignity."

"The statue must be in your arms at all times while it is out of doors and then placed carefully on the display where it is to reside until the next day."

I nodded. "I know how it is done. I've been helping Alfredo rehearse."

"We've both been helping him," Estefina said. Her arms were crossed now, and her lower lip stuck out angrily. But I couldn't keep the smile from my lips. I was going to carry Our Lady through the streets of our village for nine nights in a row. Everyone in the town would see me doing it. And my father,

also. He had promised Mother that he would be home for las celebraciones navideñas.

It was going to be a wonderful Christmas.

- 52 -

ALMA

CHAPTER 10 – MID-DECEMBER 1847
Taos, New Mexico

The winter is unusually cold, and Alma's father isn't ready to return to the valley. He seems satisfied to use reports of heavy snow in the pass and his need to talk to Carlos Beaubien to remain in Taos.

The judge is rarely there for more than twenty-four hours and Gerald spends most of his time in the parlor with Jeremiah Peabody, reminiscing about the old days as a trapper and the courting of Alma's mother. Alma often sits listening, carding wool she will probably never spin or weave. But it keeps her restlessness down and gives her an excuse to listen to the men talk.

"She was yours from the moment you told her about that bit of irrigated land she could use for her potatoes," Jeremiah says one afternoon, his eyes glinting with amusement. "She didn't even care what your Daddy was."

Gerald stiffens slightly and the old man waves his hand. "Not that I did, of course. I'd met him already and knew his worth. He was one of the best of the mountain men, even though he couldn't tell a tall tale to save his life."

Gerald grins. "My father was always a man of few words."

"And she eventually recovered from her snit when she found out who his people were."

Gerald nods. "She did." He grins wryly. "Although that was a very long winter."

Alma's hands pause. Her father's head swings toward her. "I've never forgiven myself for letting her take you children to Santa Fe in 1837, smack into that rebellion."

"That was almost ten years ago, Papa," she says. "And you didn't know there was going to be an insurrection." She grins at him. "Though I must say I was glad enough to return to the valley."

Her grandfather smiles at her. "You're certainly not much of a town girl, are you?"

"Taos is nice. I know people here, and of course, you make it home."

"The shops don't interest you? The ribbons and gimcracks at the Beaubien and Bent stores, for example?"

She smooths the wool in her lap. "I like this better. It feels more substantial, somehow."

The two men exchange a smile. Then the door opens and Andrew ushers Padre Martínez and Tomás Romero into the room. Annamaria follows close behind with coffee and bis-cochitos, her hair in its usual coil on her head and her face in its usual skeptical twist. Andrew settles in the corner with a book in his hands, though he doesn't open it.

When the greetings are over, the priest turns to Jeremiah. "We come in the hope that you might elucidate a point of Amer-ican law."

Alma's grandfather nods. "You may well know more about the question at hand than I, though I will certainly endeavor to assist you."

"Before we begin, I must inform you that this conversation is precipitated by a remark Ignacia Jaramillo made in response to a small jest of my own regarding the need for we nuevo mexicanos to stand up to the American impulse to envelop everything in their path."

"Not all of us," Gerald says mildly.

The priest nods at him. "Given your heritage, I hardly think you are wholly delighted with this invasion, since slavery persists in los Estados Unidos de América."

The other man shrugs. "My father was a freeman. I anticipate no trouble."

Jeremiah frowns at the priest. "What is it that concerns you?"

"During our interaction, Señora Jaramillo insisted that Nuevo México is part of los Estados Unidos and that my comment— I was merely joking! —encouraged insurrection." His face darkens. "Was insurrectionist!"

Tomás Romero's face is grave. "The cost of insurrection is death," he says.

The priest nods. "Sí, that is the lawful response to an illegal action against a legitimately established government. However—" He turns to Jeremiah. "The question remains as to whether the current administration here in New Mexico of which Charles Bent is governor can be considered legitimate. The United States Army holds our land as the result of an invasion during a conflict between two governments."

"A war which continues," Romero says. "The outcome remains uncertain."

The priest's eyes remain fixed on Alma's grandfather. "This is a difficult question to put to you, Don Jeremiah, since you yourself originated in the east," he says. Then he smiles. "It is a sign of our estimate of your love for our country and our esteem for your fairness of mind that we ask your opinion in this matter."

Jeremiah Peabody smooths his chin beard with one hand. "I take it that the question before us is whether Charles Bent is the head of a legitimately established government to which New Mexicans must submit or, conversely, if he represents an occupying force which may be legally resisted." He shifts in his seat, studying his visitors. "And you wish to clarify this point. May I ask why you seek to do so?"

Romero and the padre look at each other, then the Taos leader says slowly, "There is talk of action against the invader."

Gerald sits up straighter. "A counter offensive?"

The priest shrugs. "Nothing formal. There is not the manpower to do so, or, for that matter, the formal structure to organize such an action, since Manuel Armijo has fled."

"Until he returns," Romero says.

Jeremiah nods. "I have also heard rumors of a return. At the head of an army of five thousand men. Given his most recent actions, do you think it likely?"

A smile flickers across the other man's face. "El gobernador is a man of surprises."

Gerald laughs. "That's one way to put it."

The padre smiles thinly. "Regardless of the potential for Governor Armijo to resurrect his courage, the question of the legality of resistance remains."

Jeremiah considers him, looks at the bookshelf in the corner, then shakes his head. "I have no legal tomes from which to glean any wisdom on this matter," he says. "I fear it's a subject which must remain open to interpretation."

Gerald frowns. "It seems to me that the answer will depend on the loyalties of the person in question."

His father-in-law smiles slightly. "Or origins."

The priest nods. "I feared that would be your assessment, Don Jeremiah." He places his coffee cup on the small table beside his chair and laces his hands together. "These are troublous times with no easy solutions. We must all do as we must."

There's a long moment of silence, then Tomás Romero turns to Gerald. "And I must ask you, señor, if you have spoken to Carlos Beaubien about the land Armijo granted him and the others."

"I'm afraid I haven't seen Don Carlos since we last talked." Gerald glances at Alma and Andrew. "I am concerned about the situation, of course. Especially since you told me about the copper and gold."

Andrew frowns and edges toward Alma. "Gold?" he mutters in her ear as the men continue their conversation.

She nods. "Don Tomás says men from the pueblo have picked up pieces of copper and have encountered soldiers hunting gold in the streambeds."

He straightens, his eyes wide, as their father says, "I have trouble believing in the presence of gold. Certainly, I've never seen evidence of it."

"I may have, Papa," Andrew says. He looks at the others one by one, his forehead crinkling. "At least, I don't know, but it might be. I have often noticed how the creek bottoms glint in the sunlight when the water runs clear." He shakes his head. "I never dreamed it could be real gold."

"Well, when we return, you and I will have to do a little panning ourselves," Gerald says. "I doubt there's any there to speak of, but I suppose a few gold flakes wouldn't be amiss the next time your mother—" Then he stops. The others stare, startled, and then look hurriedly away. He blinks and shakes his head.

"Should we need to repair a window or something, and need cash money," he says quietly.

TERESINA

CHAPTER 11 – DECEMBER 21, 1846
Taos, New Mexico

The first few evenings of Las Posadas were difficult for me. The carved wooden statue of Our Lady was only twelve inches high, perhaps fourteen with the base. But my young arms found it heavy going.

The sixth night was easier, perhaps because I knew the procession would end at my godfather's house. Don Cornelio was often stiff with other people, but he was kind to me. I looked forward to showing him how strong and responsible I was. Also, I was wearing a new skirt Josefa had made for me. It was bright yellow and decorated with red ribbons attached meticulously in eight bright rows between the waist and hem.

We all paraded proudly through the streets, singing our songs, stopping at the designated houses to make appropriate requests, and receive the traditional responses. No one had room for Our Lady and San José. Finally, the procession ended at the Vigil casa, where hot chocolate and sugar-dusted biscochitos were spread on long wooden tables and the hand-carved benches along the wall were piled with pillows with brightly embroidered cotton covers.

Don Cornelio was nowhere to be seen in the crowded room. I maneuvered my way to my mother, who was seated on a bench between Rumalda and a young woman I didn't recognize. Her dark hair wasn't as long as my half sister's, but it was much curlier. When she turned her head to look around the room, I saw that she had light brown skin with darker splotches on her forehead and cheeks. The one on the left cheek was shaped like a heart. She smiled when she saw me, and I looked at my mother. Did I know this person?

Rumalda reached for my hand. "Teresina, come meet my friend, Alma Locke."

The newcomer smiled at me. "Hola, Teresina. I see you are still as pretty as you were four years ago."

I gave her a confused look.

"You were very tiny the last time the Lockes were in Taos," my mother said. She reached for the señorita's hand. "When Alma's dear Mama was still with us."

The smile dropped from the younger woman's eyes. "Yes."

"But now a new chapter begins," Mama said. She squeezed the señorita's hand. "I know it is very hard."

Tears glimmered in Alma's eyes. "Yes," she said again.

Rumalda turned to me. "Are you tired, pequeña?"

I shook my head.

Señorita Locke glanced at her gratefully, then smiled at me. "I saw you carrying Our Lady. That is a big responsibility, and you did it so bravely and with such grace."

I dimpled at her. "Gracias, señorita."

A violin squawked in the far corner of the room. We all turned to look. Two men with fiddles and another with a guitar were clustered together, tuning their instruments. Others were moving the tables from the center of the room.

"We are to have music!" Rumalda said with delight. "And dancing!"

As she spoke, a lanky young man with straight dark hair that hung over his forehead materialized beside me. He bowed to my mother. "Doña Ignacia," he said formally. "I bid you good evening."

"Ah, Manuel!" she said. "Buenas noches to you, as well!"

He brushed his hair out of his eyes and glanced in Alma's direction, and Mama smiled. "Alma, may I introduce a young man who has recently moved here from La Joya, there north of Chimayó?"

Señorita Locke's lips twitched upward in the semblance of a smile, but she nodded and my mother continued. "Alma, may I present Manuel Antonio Paiz, who we call Manuel because his older brother is Ysidro Antonio. Manuel, this is Alma Encarnacion Locke, of the Moreno Valley in the eastern mountains. She is the granddaughter of Jeremiah Peabody."

He brightened. "I know Señor Peabody. His house is on the road to my brother's casa. He is the New Englander with the books."

Alma smiled. "Sí, he has a few books."

"Padre Martínez says he is most wise."

Her smile broadened. At the end of the room, the musicians began playing a dance tune. Manuel looked toward them, then back to the señorita. "Would you honor me with this dance?"

She looked down, biting her lip.

"She mourns her mother," Rumalda explained. "We buried her last month."

He turned a sympathetic gaze to the orphaned girl. "Please forgive me, señorita, and accept my deepest condolences. Would you prefer to walk a bit, instead?" He brushed his hair from his eyes again, then gestured at the gathering dancers. "The room will become crowded now with merrymakers. May I escort you outside for a breath of fresh air? I would be interested to learn about your life in the mountains." He smiled. "I myself have lived always by the Río Grande and Taos is the farthest I've roamed in my travels."

She nodded and rose and took his arm, and they proceeded across the room. I leaned closer to Rumalda. "Why does her skin look like that?"

She frowned at me. "¿Que?"

I gestured toward my forehead. "The dark marks. And the heart on her cheek."

"It is a condition of the skin," my mother said. "She was born with it, poor little one."

"She is still very pretty," Rumalda said. "And one of the kindest and sweetest people I know."

My eyes found Señorita Locke and Señor Paiz. They were almost to the outer door. Then I was distracted by Rumalda's seventeen-year-old relative, Rafael Luna, who had appeared beside me. "Buenas noches, Uncle Rafael!" Rumalda said, laughing up at him.

He grinned at her, his beautiful dark eyes dancing, but they were focused more on the door than Rumalda. "Who is the curly haired beauty?"

My mother shook her head at him. "You have seen her only from the back. How do you know she is beautiful?"

He waved his hands in the air, curving them in and out. "She has una figura muy bonita."

Rumalda laughed. "You are beyond hope, old tío mío."

He put his hand on his hip and stuck his chest out, displaying the carefully ironed pleats on the front of his white shirt. "I may be your old Uncle, but I can still dance." He offered her his hand, and she hopped up to take it.

They hurried off to the center of the room, and I joined my mother on the bench. "Why does she call him 'old uncle'?" I asked. "He's only two years older than she is."

"He is her father's younger brother, so he is her uncle, but he was only two years old when she was born. When they were children together, he loved to tell her that she had to obey him because he was her uncle. They've been teasing each other about it ever since."

I turned to watch the dancers. "It's silly. And he's a flirt. I hope Señorita Locke has nothing to do with him. I like Manuel Antonio much better. He seems very kind."

Mother smiled and absently patted my shoulder as she watched the dancers. They swung vigorously through the movements of the waltz, then the music ended, and the players took a break. The door to the courtyard opened, and Manuel and Alma came in, followed by the broad shoulders of Don Cornelio.

"Godfather!" I cried. I hopped off the bench and ran to him. He smiled down at me. "Is it appropriate to kiss the lady who carried Our Lady this evening?" he asked gravely.

I nodded eagerly and he bent to kiss my cheek, then swung me into his arms. "Come, let us go to your mother."

When we got to her, we also found Josefa, Benigna Lee, and Luz Beaubien. Josefa sat down next to my mother, but Benigna smiled and reached for me. "You carried Our Lady most excellently this evening," she said, lifting me from my godfather's grasp.

"Oui," Luz agreed. "I would not have expected it of one so petite."

I wrinkled my nose at her and smoothed my skirt. "Petite? Is that a French word?"

"C'est français, oui" Luz said. "You honor your heritage by processing with Our Lady, I honor mine with mon vocabulaire."

Don Cornelio laughed. "Your store of words seems to have increased since your marriage."

She lifted her chin at him. "My husband's grandfather—"

"Was French. Yes, I am aware that Lucien Maxwell is French Canadian." He shrugged. "As is your father."

"He is a seigneur. He would have had peasants working the land for him, if he'd stayed in New France. It is a title of some standing, even if he does persist in owning a shop."

He regarded her indulgently, smiled, and turned away. She glowered at him and looked pointedly at Benigna and Josefa. "Shall we walk?" Her face brightened. "Did I tell you? Narciso will be home from college soon!"

Josefa smiled in response, but her eyes were on Don Cornelio as he looked down at my mother. "I believe Señor Vigil has family news for us," she told Luz. She extracted me from Benigna's arms and placed me in her lap. "I will stay here for the moment."

We all watched the others walk off, then Don Cornelio turned to Mama. "There is news from Santa Fe."

She gave him a wary look. "Yes?"

"Before I begin, let me assure you your husband is well."

She stiffened. Josefa scooted over on the bench, to allow him to sit, and he wedged himself between her and my mother, who held her hand out to me. I slipped from Josefa's lap and tucked myself under Mama's arm.

"A conspiracy of insurrection has been uncovered —"

Mother's hand flew to her mouth. Don Cornelio nodded soberly. "Some of the most prominent men in Nuevo México were involved. But now all has been discovered and they have been detained. Thanks to your husband's connections and swift actions, Nuevo México is secure once again."

Mother closed her eyes in relief. I looked from her to Don Cornelio's sober face. He was watching me now. I frowned. "If there is no danger, why are you sad?"

"I have bad news for you, pequeña," he said gently. "Because of the conspiracy and the reports he must now prepare to send to those in Washington City, your father will not be able to attend the feast of the nativity with you." He nodded at my ribbon-decorated skirt. "He will not be here to see you in Las Posadas."

"Not at all?"

Don Cornelio shook his head. "I'm sorry, pequeña. I know you wanted very much for him to be here."

I nodded and pressed my face into my mother's shoulder. She patted my arm. "You have done so excellently this year, perhaps the ladies will request your services again when you are six," she said. "Your father is sure to be here next year."

I shook my head, smearing my tears on her silk dress. "It won't be the same."

My mother patted me again and turned back to Don Cornelio. "But all is well now? There is no further talk of rebellion? They have rooted out the leaders and locked them safely away?"

He smiled gravely and patted her arm. "All is well. He is simply delayed."

ALMA

CHAPTER 12 – CHRISTMAS DAY, 1846
Taos, New Mexico

Alma wakes on Christmas morning with a sense of dread. She'd attended most of the Las Posadas processions as well as the Christmas Eve midnight mass and all the activity has kept her memories at bay, but now they threaten to overwhelm her. Her mother, face bright as she lights the candles on the tree she's coerced Ramón and Gerald into setting up in the weaving room. The anticipation of the gifts each member of the family has prepared in secret over the past weeks. Helping Ramón prepare the annual feast of rich posole and roast pork followed by les natillas, the egg and milk pudding that is his signature dessert.

Alma closes her eyes. It will be so different this year. Without her mother. Without Ramón. Suddenly, she wants nothing more than to see his weathered brown face and kind eyes, feel his sympathetic gaze. If she can't have her mother—

There's a tap on her door and Andrew sticks his head in the room. "Grandfather is asking for you." As she swings her feet from the bed and reaches for her shawl, he adds, "We have company. You'll need to make yourself presentable."

Then he's gone, and she runs her fingers through her curls, trying vainly to straighten them, and hurries into her clothes.

When she reaches the parlor, she finds a long-faced young man she's never seen before with her father and grandfather, and Andrew poking at the fire with a stick.

They all turn as she enters. "Ah, there you are," her grandfather says. "We've been invited to attend the Christmas dances at Taos Pueblo today." He gestures toward the stranger. "This is Juan Pacheco of the pueblo, sent by Señor Romero to escort us, if we would like to attend." His voice trails off.

She glances at her father, who looks away. Andrew straightens from the fire. "We've never been to one before," he says.

It's true. They've been to the pueblo, but not the dances. Alma doesn't really want to go, but it's better than staying here with her memories. She nods a reluctant agreement. Anamaria comes in with a tray of steaming coffee and cups. "You must first take sustenance," she says. She scowls at the newcomer. "A message yesterday would have been most timely."

He looks at her sheepishly. "Sí, madre."

Alma looks from one to the other. There is a family resemblance around the slitted eyes and high cheekbones. "You are mother and son?"

"For my sins," Anamaria says, but her face softens as she smiles at the newcomer. She turns to Alma's grandfather. "The breakfast will be ready en un momento, señor."

"You will attend also, mamá?" Juan Pacheco asks. She nods abruptly and goes out. He clicks his tongue disparagingly and shakes his head, a smile on his lips.

Andrew drops into a chair near the fire and looks at his grandfather. "I thought she was Spanish."

"There is much intermarriage between the pueblo and the village," Jeremiah says mildly.

The Taos man nods. "It is so." He clicks his tongue. "Though the grandfather of mi madre is of the savage tribes, which makes her la genízara."

"Ah," Andrew says.

"Many here in the Taos Valley are of mixed race," Gerald says. "Just as your mother is—" He pauses, looks away, then at Juan Pacheco. "Suzanna's mother was half French and half Navajo."

Andrew runs his hands through his curly blond hair. "Not that I look it."

"You are one of a kind," Alma says teasingly, and they all laugh, finish their coffee, and move to the kitchen when Anamaria calls them.

After they've eaten all they can hold, she hustles them out the door. The village of Taos is starting to wake from its Christmas Eve revels. The nutty scent of burning piñon logs fills the air. As they pass the entrance to the plaza, Luz Beaubien appears.

"Bonjour," she says to the men, and Andrew and Alma roll their eyes at each other. She nods to them majestically, then continues on up the street as Jeremiah and Gerald stop to exchange greetings with Sheriff Lee and the prefect, Cornelio Vigil.

"You are all out early," Lee says jovially. He pushes his hat back from his forehead and surveys Anamaria and her son, his face a mixture of amusement and query.

"It's a good day for walking," Jeremiah says mildly.

Alma looks up. The sky is brilliantly blue. Puffy clouds glow in the sunlight, more decorative than threatening. The air is crisp, but not truly cold.

"An excellent day for a Pueblo dance," her grandfather adds.

"It may be a little cold for watching, though," Lee says. He grins at Anamaria's son. "I imagine there'll be a little Taos lightning flowing to keep everyone warm. I guess Simeon Turley has been busy up that way."

The Taos man gives him a level look, then glances away, but Anamaria scowls at the sheriff. "Alcohol on Christmas Day!" she sniffs. "The idea!"

Cornelio Vigil and Lee exchange amused glances. "You are on your way to the pueblo?" Vigil asks the Lockes.

"We've been invited by Señor Tomás Romero," Andrew tells him.

Vigil and Lee exchange another look, this one less amused. The sheriff turns to Jeremiah. "I hear he and the padre have been consulting you about American law."

"Yes, that is correct."

"He might want to remember that it now takes precedence here."

Jeremiah raises an eyebrow. "Has peace been declared?"

The lawman looks at Vigil, who shakes his head slightly. Lee shrugs. "Well, I'm here and I'm in charge of administering American law," he says. "We're not attending the dance up there for the pleasure of it. Someone's been stealing corn from a hacienda nearby. We expect to identify the culprits responsible real soon now."

Alma's grandfather frowns. "I do hope you're not planning to make an arrest today."

Lee chuckles. "And stir up a whole nest of hornets? No, it'll have to wait a bit." He glances at Cornelio Vigil. "Though I will take care of it before we leave for Santa Fe."

Jeremiah cocks an eye at him, then at the snow-covered mountains above the town. "You're heading there soon?"

"The roads south aren't too bad just yet," Vigil says. "The new year has not yet begun."

The snows always seem to descend in earnest in January. The group shares a chuckle, then Vigil and Lee turn and head up the road toward the pueblo, Alma and her family behind them. After a while Vigil drops back to walk beside Anamaria and her son, and Lee settles in beside Jeremiah. "I reckon your conversation with Romero had something to do with the new administration," the sheriff says.

"You could say that."

"Whether the war is over or not, these people need to remember we have judges now, not alcaldes. People who misbehave will be jailed until the next court session and given a proper sentence. No more running free after the alcalde taps their wrist with one hand while accepting bribes from their relatives with the other."

Jeremiah frowns. "You've lived in this region over twenty years, Luis. You know that what appears to outsiders to be a bribe is actually mutual support and care from the community at large. Gifts to the alcalde free him to attend to governance instead of constant monitoring of his flocks and fields. Also, it is well to remember that everyone here is related to everyone else. It would be difficult to find a malefactor who doesn't have an upright family member who actively supports the alcalde's work."

"Call it what you will," Lee says. "That's all done with now." He adjusts his hat lower on his forehead. "As sheriff, I receive a salary. That makes your so-called 'mutual support' unnecessary."

Alma frowns. There's a tension here that needs to be dissipated. "Did you say you were going to Santa Fe?" she asks Lee.

He nods, a look of satisfaction in his face. "Vigil and Pablo Jaramillo and I have business with the new government."

She's about to ask about the conditions of the roads for wagon traffic when Benigna, Josefa, and Rumalda emerge from the street on the left, from the direction of the Bent casa.

"Buenos días!" the girls say as they get closer. They make the rounds of the group, greeting each one with a sideways hug. Alma sees her father hesitate, then solemnly submit and pat Josefa's arm as she releases him.

"Juan Pacheco!" Rumalda says. "How are you? And Anamaria! You are well?"

"Well enough. What brings you out so early this morning?"

The three young women look at each other and smile. "The children are fussy today, and sad because their father remained in Santa Fe," Josefa says. "We thought it best to leave them to their mother's ministrations."

"She's telling them stories of how she and Charles met and how big Bent's Fort is, and the size of the house he grew up in," Rumalda says. She laughs. "They are interesting stories, but I've heard them before."

Benigna smiles at Anamaria's son. "When we heard that Los Matachines is to be performed at the pueblo today, we decided that we'd prefer to watch that instead." She hesitates. "If we're allowed?"

He smiles and extends an arm, which she takes while her father watches with narrowed eyes. She smiles at him. "I will pay close attention, Papa, so I can describe it all in great detail to José when he returns home."

The sheriff gives her a sideways look but doesn't respond. They all move on toward the Taos Pueblo. They can see Luz in the distance, but she doesn't turn back to wait for them.

The fields are coated with snow, but the road is dry. Birds flit among the branches of the cottonwoods lining the irrigation ditches. Alma feels her heart lift in spite of the knot of dull pain in her chest.

"How your mother would have loved this," her father says in a low voice, and she reaches for his arm.

Others are also converging on the pueblo. As Alma and her father reach the low western wall anchored by the massive adobe church in the compound's left corner, Manuel Paiz appears. His older brother Ysidro is just behind him with his wife and two small children. Everyone lines up to file through the gate in the wall. Two men flank it, watching. They're wrapped in long white blankets, and they exude a calm command. There is no doubt that they will bar anyone who looks like they might cause trouble.

Alma nods politely to them and the taller one gives her an appraising look. There's a jagged scar on his cheek. He jerks his chin at her, motioning her into the compound, and she moves forward, her father behind her. "Do you remember this?" he asks.

She nods slowly, taking in the tall church with its bell tower and the massive adobe housing units. There's one to her left, behind the church, and another off to the right. They're five stories high, each level stepped back perhaps ten feet from the one below. The resulting terraces are crowded with people peering at a cleared space in the big square below.

"I had forgotten how large it all is," Alma says. She gestures toward the little river that flows between them and the housing structure on the right. Sunlight sparkles on the ice along its edges. "And the beauty of the Río Pueblo."

A drum begins to sound; a slow, deep throb. Alma's father looks toward their escort, who's bending over Anamaria, talking into her ear. Her mouth is pursed in disapproval. Then she shakes free of him. "Remember your guests," she says. "Your escort duties are not yet complete."

Juan's face twitches in irritation, then smooths as he turns to Alma's grandfather. "Señor," he says. "Will you come this way? Don Tomás has a space prepared for you—." Then he pauses uncertainly and clicks his tongue. "It is on the second level of North House."

Jeremiah Peabody smiles at him. "I am still agile enough to ascend a ladder or two." He glances at Andrew, whose head is swiveling back and forth, taking everything in. "I wouldn't want to spoil anyone's view."

Juan nods and they follow him across the big square, the Lees and the Paiz family behind them. They all clamber up the heavy wooden ladders, make their way through the little crowd on the ledge formed by the first building, then climb to the next level.

Tomás Romero greets them there, his face lighting up at the sight of Anamaria. "Doña," he says. "It is an honor to see you here. Your son has been especially helpful to me recently."

Juan clicks his tongue self-disparagingly and glances toward the Paiz family. The men have lifted the children onto their shoulders, as a precaution against attempts at the wall's low parapet. The Taos leader moves toward them. "You are wise to take such safeguards," he tells the two men. "Although the fall is not a long one, and someone is always on watch against such an event."

The youthful Manuel Paiz smiles at him a little apologetically. "Thank you for allowing us to join you today."

"You are always welcome. However, I must leave you to attend to my duties." He turns back to Jeremiah Peabody and smiles. "I stayed only to welcome my old friend." The drums below shift their rhythm, sharpening and deepening at the same time. He glances toward the square. "Forgive me, but I must bid you farewell for the time being."

Alma moves to the parapet to watch him go, noting how respectfully those on the next level greet him. As he reaches the ground, Sheriff Lee and Cornelio Vigil approach, shepherding Luz, Rumalda, and Josefa. The Taos leader stops to speak to them, then gestures toward the upper level of the building. Josefa looks up and smiles, her eyes bright, and Alma waves.

Vigil looks doubtfully at the ladder. After all, he's a tall and thick-bodied man. But Tomás Romero says something else, and Vigil laughs and nods and gestures at the girls to make the climb. There's a grin on Romero's face as he turns away. Alma knows it by the set of his shoulders. She chuckles and moves to the top of the ladder to greet the newcomers.

CHAPTER 13 – CHRISTMAS 1846
Taos Pueblo, New Mexico

The tempo of the drums changes as Luz steps from the ladder and straightens her skirts. Benigna and Josefa follow her, and the girls all move to the edge of the parapet. The rectangular dance ground below is ringed with observers from the Pueblo and nearby villages. Two large wooden chairs, their seats well cushioned and their backs hung with intricately designed wool rugs, are positioned at the near end, facing the square.

The drumbeats change again. A violin begins to play in the distance, a pulsing rhythm that echoes and enhances the drums. Two musicians appear and move to the right, next to the drummers at the far end of the dancing ground. The pace of the tune increases. Two dancers enter the square side by side, a tall man and a little girl dressed in white buckskin, her face tight with concentration.

"This performance is always a wonder to me," Josefa says. "I wish Kit was here to see it. He knows so many of these people."

"Not that he would know who he was watching," Luz says.

She has a point. The fringe on the man's headdress hangs over his eyes, obscuring his face. His mouth is covered by a finely woven wool scarf.

"He is el Monarca, king of the dance and the little girl is la Malinche, symbol of purity," Josefa tells Alma, who nods, her eyes fixed on the figures below.

They settle into the thrones at the head of the dancing ground and more dancers come in. There are twelve of them, two rows of men wearing tall miter-shaped headdresses with long fringe in front and ribbons dangling behind. These are the Matachines, for whom the dance is named.

Each man carries a gourd rattle in his right hand and a short wooden pitchfork-shaped object in his left. They step in unison, shaking their rattles and lifting and lowering the pitchforks in time to the music.

Josefa leans forward. "Look, here come los abuelos! How funny they look!"

The two men in question are dressed in ragged clothes several sizes too big for them. They wear hoods with holes cut out for their eyes and mouths. One of them has long, wild hair and a big belly that he holds from underneath as if showing it off to the crowd. Alma lifts an eyebrow.

Josefa grins. "That is la abuela, the grandmother. She's supposed to be with child."

"But it's actually a man," Benigna says. "Malinche is the only female in this dance."

Luz laughs. "Because a man can't symbolize innocence." She looks at Alma. "The other one is el abuelo, the grandfather, of course."

The two columns of Matachines are in place now, facing the seated king and girl as they maintain a steady step in time to the music. The abuelos dart among them, pushing the dancers into or out of their places and twitching the ribbons that hang down their backs.

"And here comes el Toro," Luz says.

Josefa shakes her head sympathetically. "Poor creature."

Rumalda grins. "It's only a dance."

The newcomer is draped in an animal hide and wears a head-dress with buffalo horns attached to its crown. He leans forward on two sticks that represent the front feet of a bull. Alma shakes her head. "He looks uncomfortable!"

The bull makes a roaring sound and prances up and down between the columns of dancers, then maneuvers into position behind the two thrones. La Malinche turns and smiles at him and he growls at her. Alma is close enough to see the girl's eyes widen before she turns back to face los Matachines.

El abuelo, the beggarly old man yells, "Vuelta!" and the dancing men make a quarter turn, keeping in step. This goes on for a bit, then la Malinche stands hesitantly and the dancer playing the pregnant old woman shuffles up and takes her hand. Together they weave in and out between the dancing Matachines.

While they're doing this, the bull, still behind the thrones, lets out a bellow or two. But most of the action is on the dancing ground, where el abuelo capers along the sidelines, yelling "vuelto!" at intervals. In response, the Matachines make precise quarter turns, never missing a step.

Luz moves impatiently. "This event is always exactly the same," she grumbles.

"And yet always different," Josefa says. "The bull this year has quite a fine voice."

"It certainly carries," Benigna says. She glances at Luz. "His timing seems a little different, as well. I think he's bellowing more often."

"It's becoming très monotone," Luz says. "Let me know when something exciting happens." She moves away, toward the back of the terrace, where someone has placed a row of up-ended blocks of wood, and seats herself on the largest one.

Don Cornelio crosses to sit beside her. Alma turns back to the dance. Malinche and the dancer playing the old woman have returned to the throne and the little girl and el Monarca are doing some kind of elaborate hand ritual.

Then El Monarca rises and dances down the corridor between the Matachines and back again. When he turns to make another pass, they raise their arms, forming a canopy over his head. As he goes by a third time, they kneel in his wake and stretch their arms into the space between the two rows. To return, he has to hop over their hands or risk stepping on them. As Alma holds her breath, he hops all the way down and then back again to his seat.

Luz has returned to the parapet. "They do this every year," she complains. The bull bellows again, more strongly this time, and she grimaces. "That's the only difference."

The others ignore her. Andrew, Manuel Paiz, and Juan Pacheco have joined the girls at the wall. "What are the little wooden pitchforks called?" Alma asks no one in particular.

Manuel Paiz moves closer. "Those are palmas."

"Like a palm branch?"

"I suppose so." He looks at Juan, who shrugs, nods, and says, "They may symbolize many things. The Christian trinity. Quetzalcoatl. The swords of the Spanish."

"Quetzalcoatl?" Alma's grandfather has joined them now. Her father is sitting next to Cornelio Vigil, deep in conversation.

"The god of Mexico," Juan says.

Jeremiah Peabody nods. "How is it that the palma represents him?"

"He is the lord of air, water, and land."

"Ah, the three fingers. That's very interesting."

"I have always known them to represent the Trinity," Luz says.

Juan clicks his tongue. "That is one interpretation."

"The Spanish one." Rumalda grins at her. "As well as the French, I suppose."

Luz gives her a narrow-eyed look, as if she suspects the other girl of mocking her. When Rumalda smiles back innocently, Luz moves to the back of the ledge and settles beside Alma's father. Cornelio Vigil is now talking to Sheriff Lee, on his other side.

Alma turns back to the dance. The Matachines are back on their feet and dancing in place. El Monarca leads la Malinche onto the dancing ground. El Toro's bellows are so loud that Alma can barely hear when el abuelo shouts "Vuelta!"

The dancers turn, the pretend bull bellows, and the tall man and little girl move among the Matachines, pulling on their arms, and pushing them from behind to move them into new positions. The old lady dancer capers up and down the sidelines, shouting "¡No servirá de nada! It will do no good!" at the king and girl.

Juan Pacheco leans toward Alma. "The actions of el Monarca and la Malinche represent the tide of change," he says. "See how they move the dancers around without seeking permission? As if they are toys to be rearranged at a child's whim?"

Alma nods. El Toro bellows again. La abuela screeches "It will do no good!" from the other end of the dancing ground. When los Matachines have all been rearranged, el Monarca and la Malinche dance back to their thrones and sit down. There's a long pause, then the music changes and the two columns of dancers step out of their positions and begin weaving between each other.

Josefa leans forward, eyes intent. "I have never been able to follow how they do this," she says. She turns to Alma. Over the bellows of the fake bull she shouts, "Watch where they end up! It will be exactly where they were before they were rearranged!"

Alma leans out, gazing intently, but she hasn't paid enough attention to the dancers' original positions. She'll have to take Josefa's word for it.

When all the Matachines are back in their original spots, facing the thrones as they dance, the old woman capers into the space in front of el Monarca. "That's what happens when you try to change us!" she yells. "¡Nosotros sobrevivimos! We survive!"

There's a smattering of applause from the crowd. Manuel and his brother exchange glances as Juan Pacheco snorts in approval. Alma looks at Anamaria, who stands at the far end of the parapet. Her face is tired and grim.

The next phase of the dance begins. El Monarca descends and sets up a tall pole in the center of the dancing ground. Long ribbons flutter from the top. Los Matachines begin to dance again, catching the bright strands and weaving them into an elaborate design. El Toro bellows again and again, steadily increasing in volume. When the ribbons are all secure, the dancers back away and continue to dance, facing the pole.

Then the music stops. In the silence, the bull bellows even louder, but everyone ignores him. All eyes are on la abuela, who capers along the edges of the dance area, hollering rude comments. She does a summersault at the far end of the square, then dances a jig in front of a short stocky man with a scowl on his face. Suddenly she jerks to a stop and bends down.

"¡Mierda!" she screeches as she pretends to scrape something off the bare dirt. "It's pure gold!"

Alma stifles a laugh. "Did she just say what I think she did?"

"She did." Her father comes up behind her, then turns to Josefa. "What has he done to deserve such recognition?"

Josefa studies the scowling face at the other end of the square. "I think he's the one who's been providing information to los americanos about various people around Taos."

"They say he's doing it for money," Rumalda adds.

Manuel Paiz nods. "Yes, that's him. El traidor."

His older brother gives him a warning look and turns to Gerald. "It is said he makes much of little as a way to increase the coins he receives."

"And he is from the pueblo?"

"Sí," Juan Pacheo says, scowling at the man below. "We have lost much of our harmony since los soldados americanos arrived."

"And yet none of them are here in the Taos Valley."

"Poison spreads far beyond the location where it first enters the body. We must act soon if we are to protect our traditions."

"We must rebel," Manuel mutters. At least, that's what Alma thinks he says. When she glances at him, he looks away.

Alma studies the crowd below. The drums start up again, the violins following, and the Matachines begin unwinding their earlier creation. The bull bellows again.

"He certainly has a strong voice," Josefa chuckles.

Sheriff Lee has joined them now. Ysidro Paiz appears not to have seen him. "Next year, they'll need to replace those buffalo horns with a set from a Texas longhorn," he says.

Lee gives him a sharp look. "You'd best watch your tongue."

Ysidro smiles blandly. "But this United States of America which is now in control of me and my countrymen, is it not a land of free speech?"

Lee glowers at him. Cornelio Vigil has risen and come up behind the two men. He leans toward Ysidro. "It is not wise to annoy those in power."

Juan Pacheco clicks his tongue and gestures toward the scene below. "This dance reminds us that those in power do not always remain so."

As the two men stare at him, there's a sudden shout below, then a louder bellow than any before.

Luz has joined Don Cornelio. She stands on tiptoe to see over Alma's shoulder. "Enfin!" she says. "El Toro begins!"

The bull dances awkwardly up and down the space between the columns of Matachines, who now face each other. The bull tosses its head and lets out one bellow after the other. The grandparent figures dash in and out, flapping their ragged arms and yelling at it. The grandfather has a whip, which he flourishes vigorously, though the tip doesn't actually hit anyone.

"This part always lasts too long," Josefa murmurs.

Luz elbows past her and places her hands on the parapet. "It's the only interesting part in the entire thing."

"How bloodthirsty you are!" Rumalda teases.

Alma gives her a puzzled look, then turns back to the dance. El Toro is on the ground, the grandmother figure sitting on his chest as the bull helplessly waves his stick arms in the air. The grandfather figure has dropped his whip and is swinging a big wooden knife, thrusting downward, and making slashing gestures. The bull bellows one last time and goes still, pretending to die.

El abuelo rises and swings his pretend knife at el Toro's groin, then fumbles under the bull's costume and pulls out a large leather bag that's cinched in the middle to create a bulge on each side.

"Is that supposed to be—?" Alma can't say it. She's seen bulls castrated before, but this is something else entirely.

"It is," Luz confirms, laughing. "C'est drôle."

The grandfather dancer opens the bag and begins pulling out handfuls of silver and throwing them into the crowd. Everyone laughs and grabs for the coins.

While this is going on, la abuela has dropped to the ground and begun writhing in mock agony. El abuelo flings the money bag aside, rushes to her, and flaps his arms in alarm. Then he suddenly bends over and pulls a cloth doll from beneath the old woman's skirts. The crowd cheers, Luz laughs, and the musicians increase the beat of their music.

The grandparent figures rise and dance between the Matachines to the thrones, where they display the "baby" to the king and little girl, then dance off. La abuela moves along the edge of the crowd, showing off her child, and el abuelo turns to los Matachines. "Vuelta!" he yells.

They all turn to face the two thrones. After a few minutes, the king and the little girl rise from their seats. They each move to the head of a line of dancers, and everyone begins to dance out of the square in perfect time.

And then it's over. Alma watches until they all disappear, then turns away from the parapet. She's oddly drained. As if she's been dancing through the steps of the multi-layered ritual herself.

Or so focused on it that she's lost connection with those around her. She shakes her head, pulling herself back to the terrace. Almost everyone else has descended to the square. Sheriff Lee and Cornelio Vigil are already halfway across the dancing ground, hunting their prey.

Juan Pacheco and the Paiz brothers are still on the terrace, in the far corner with their heads together. Anamaria stands next to the ladder, watching them. Alma moves toward her. "What does it all mean?" she asks.

The housekeeper gestures toward her son and the others. "They told you."

"And the baby?"

Anamaria shrugs. "Life renews itself? We will go on, despite everything?"

Alma nods, still feeling dazed, and steps onto the ladder.

"Or perhaps it means that all is not as simple as it seems."

Alma pauses on the first rung, staring at the housekeeper with her perfectly coiled braid around her head. She thinks of Grandfather Locke. Her mother. "Or that death comes to us all," she says. "And nothing lasts forever."

The housekeeper gives her a sharp look, then turns to her son and his friends.

Alma descends to her waiting family.

TERESINA

CHAPTER 14 – JANUARY 6, 1847
Taos, New Mexico

I was so excited that Wednesday morning. Josefa and Rumalda planned to attend the service celebrating Our Lord's Epiphany and they had invited Estefina and me to go with them. Mother watched our preparations with bemusement and followed us to the outer gate, where Benigna and Alma waited for us. "Say a special prayer of thanksgiving while we are there, to celebrate the news your father has sent," Mama said as she reached to close the gate.

Señorita Locke looked at me. "There is news from Santa Fe?"

I nodded, trying to suppress my need to hop up and down with excitement. "Father is coming home!"

Rumalda laughed and took my hand. "Only for a visit." She smiled at Alma. "Buenos días. Yes, it is true. He writes to say he will be here within the next fortnight."

"In time for Alfredo's birthday," Estefina said.

"Luz will be pleased," Josefa added.

Benigna gave her a puzzled look.

"Narciso Beaubien is to accompany him."

"Oh! She will be glad!" Benigna slid a glance toward Alma. "And you will have another beau to add to your quiver."

"¿Que?"

"In addition to Manuel Paiz." She grinned at Rumalda. "I also have heard that your uncle, Rafael Luna, has been asking about her."

Alma frowned and looked away.

"Don't tease her," Josefa said. She touched Alma's arm. "Though it is true that you have excited a certain amount of discussion in town. A new pretty girl is always a topic of interest."

Alma's hand went to her left cheek. "Pretty?"

"There you go, fishing for compliments!" Benigna laughed. She linked arms with Josefa and reached for Alma's hand. "We're going to be late for mass!"

We lingered after the service, lighting a candle of thanksgiving and sharing our good news with our neighbors. Some of them were delighted for us, while others went quiet and only nodded politely. I was standing between Rumalda and Alma and about to ask Rumalda why these people responded as they did when Rafael Luna appeared.

"Buenos días, señorita," he said to Alma. "It has been a long while since we met."

She half turned toward him, then looked away with a flustered expression on her face. Behind us, Benigna giggled.

Alma took my hand and moved away. "Buenos días, señor," she said over her shoulder. "Come, Teresina. Did you wish to light a candle of your own?"

I nodded eagerly.

"And why do you light a candle?" Rafael asked me as he looked at Alma.

"Father is coming home!" I told him.

"But only for a visit," Estefina interposed.

I nodded sadly and Alma smiled down at me. "A father is a splendid thing, and visits are to be treasured."

"I wish he was staying."

"He is an important man, pequeña," Rafael said. He glanced at Alma again. "You should be proud of him."

Estefina sniffed. "She thinks only of what she wants."

Rumalda frowned at her. "It is not polite to criticize others for their feelings."

Rafael grinned at Rumalda. "Yes, you should listen to your sister," he told Estefina. "She is full of wisdom because she is so much older than you."

"She's a grown lady with a husband," I pointed out.

"She has a husband; I'm not sure she's a grown lady," he said. Then he looked at Alma again. "Though she is certainly old enough to be married."

The church door opened and Padre Martínez came in, blinking his eyes against the sudden darkness. He moved toward us. "It is good to see you lingering at your prayers," he said jovially, with a wink at Rafael. He turned to Josefa. "I understand that your sister Ignacia's amante intends to pay us the honor of a visit."

Tía Josefa looked at him steadily. "Her lover? Do you mean the governor? Yes, he hopes to be here to celebrate the anniversary of his son's birth."

The padre crossed himself. "May he arrive safely and return in good health."

Rumalda's eyes narrowed. "Is there a reason to fear he won't do so?"

Rafael moved slightly, as if to break the tension between her and the priest, but the padre raised a placating hand. "I spoke as I would of any official who God sees fit to place over us."

"I hope you pray for his safety as fervently as you did for Governor Armijo's," Josefa said gravely.

The priest turned to her. "¡Por supuesto!" he said. "Of course!"

ALMA

CHAPTER 15 – JANUARY 7, 1847
Taos, New Mexico

Carlos Beaubien is a short, thin man who carries himself with an assurance that makes him seem larger than he actually is. Perhaps it's his early training as a priest. Or it could be because, as Alma's grandfather once put it, he knows more Latin and Greek than the rest of New Mexico's inhabitants combined.

Or so it's said. As Alma settles beside her brother on the cushioned bench in the Beaubien casa and studies the judge and her father in their carved chairs by the fire, she wonders how Beaubien's language skills compare to Padre Martínez's.

But that's irrelevant to the discussion at hand. Luz comes in, carrying a tray of coffee and biscochitos, distributes them, then places the tray on an American-made mahogany side table near the door and sinks onto a set of nearby wool-covered cushions. She gives Alma a conspiratorial look and Alma suppresses a grin. Luz may be here only on her father's sufferance, but Alma and her brother have been brought along as both exhibits and witnesses.

Her father is focused on the judge. "I want my children to have a place to call their own after I'm gone," he says.

Beaubien waves a hand. "That goes without saying."

Gerald sips his coffee and gazes into the fire. "Recent events have reminded me how fragile life can be."

The other man nods. "Yes, of course. I was sorry to hear of the loss of your wife." He looks at Luz, who straightens a little. "My daughter tells me Suzanna was buried with all the honors the village could accord her."

"Yes." Gerald turns to smile at Luz. "I was grateful for her presence, as well as that of the other young women in town." He glances toward the bench. "As were my daughter and son."

Carlos Beaubien swings toward Andrew and Alma. "It is a hard thing to lose a mother at such a young age."

Alma studies him. He's saying all the right things, but he seems disengaged. There's a reserve in the blue eyes and narrow face. He leans to place his coffee cup on the floor beside his chair, pushes his thin, light brown hair away from his forehead, then settles back in his seat.

He folds his hands in his lap. "I cannot make a unilateral decision regarding the disposition of the grant," he says formally. "In fact, any record of deed I give you at this time would be invalid without the signatures of all the parties involved. Unfortunately, under the current circumstances, not all those signatures are readily obtainable." He gives Alma's father a sharp look. "You understand."

Gerald settles his own cup on the floor, then straightens, his eyes on the judge's face. "You, Bent, and Guadalupe Miranda are all still in the country."

Beaubien nods, hesitates, then says reluctantly. "We must consult all the owners."

"There is another?" Gerald asks mildly.

Beaubien looks away. "Manuel Armijo may have a small interest in the matter."

"I had hoped that was only a rumor," Alma's father says gravely. "It puts the legality of the entire land grant in question."

Beaubien's head turns sharply. "Are you a lawyer now, or have you been discussing this with your father-in-law?"

Gerald shakes his head. "Neither. But the idea that a governor can give land to petitioners and then take some of it for himself seems questionable, at best."

"That isn't—"

Gerald makes a small brushing gesture with his hand. "In any case, no one knows where Armijo is at the moment." He stops and looks inquiringly at Beaubien, who shakes his head.

"Somewhere in Mexico," he says. "Or so I'm told."

Gerald nods. "Although he may be headed back to Santa Fe at the head of any number of troops, if the rumors I've heard have any basis in fact." Then he shrugs. "Of course, for all we know, he never made it to Chihuahua or Durango or wherever he fled."

Beaubien nods slowly. "In that case, the courts will adjudicate his estate."

"Which court? American or Mexican?"

"American, of course."

"Has the U.S. Congress agreed to that? Until the current conflict ends, isn't New Mexico still technically under Mexican law?"

Beaubien spreads his hands, palms up. "It's occupied territory."

"So it's under military jurisdiction." Gerald looks away, gazing up at the latillas, the slender, carefully arranged poles that form the room's ceiling. "I wonder what the American military leader here would think about the fact that one of his judges had a business relationship with the former governor of the occupied territory which was not disclosed at the time of his appointment."

Beaubien is fully engaged now. His narrow jaw twitches. "And why should you think the colonel is unaware of the arrangements related to the grant?"

Gerald's gray eyes are slightly amused. "It seems unlikely, since you haven't been particularly forthcoming to me. And I am personally concerned, since Juan Ramón Chavez and I have a right of occupancy which precedes the date Armijo granted the land." He leans back, studying the other man. "Of course, there's also the issue of who would be responsible for hearing such a case, if it went to court. It wouldn't be yourself, of course."

"No, it would be one of the other judges."

"So Ramón and I would have to go to Santa Fe? That's an expensive proposition."

"It would undoubtedly be adjudicated during a regularly scheduled session here in Taos." Beaubien moves restlessly. "That's how it's structured now. The courts go to the people, not the people to the court." He pauses, straightens a little. "In fact, I'm leaving tomorrow for a session in Tierra Amarilla."

Gerald nods. "That's a refreshing change. And necessary now that the power of the alcaldes has been restricted by the new administration. What portion of the grant did you say was assigned to Manuel Armijo? Some place up in the mountains? Taos Pueblo's holy lake, for example?"

"No, he has no specific portion."

"That's good to hear," Gerald says. "I wouldn't want any confusion about the boundaries of the land Ramón and I have been working these last twenty years."

Beaubien gives him a sharp look. "Eighteen and a half."

Gerald's lips quirk. "You remember."

"Of course. You married that pretty little Suzanna Peabody and headed into the hills." Carlos Beaubien shakes his head. "We all thought you were crazy."

Gerald grins. "So did Suzanna." Then his smile fades. He shakes his head. "I still can't believe—"

Beaubien makes a sympathetic sound, then says, "Are you certain you wish to return?"

Alma's eyes narrow.

Gerald nods toward her and her brother. "I'm not a wealthy man. That land is all I have to leave them."

"And Ramón Chavez?"

"He was Suzanna's godfather and also Alma's."

Beaubien turns toward the children and Alma nods. Sharing a godfather with a parent is unusual, but then, they aren't Catholic. It's purely a personal thing.

Gerald goes on. "These children are the reason I want some protection for that land. It wouldn't matter to Ramón and me, but it will for them."

"You mentioned boundaries." Beaubien stretches his feet toward the fire. "To establish anything certain, the land will need to be marked in the traditional way." He glances at Gerald to see if he understands.

The other man nods. "I can identify the locations of those corners whenever you call upon me to do so. In fact, I can draw you a map and give you a physical description right now."

Beside the door at the other end of the room, Luz rises from her cushions and lifts the tray from the little table. The cups rattle and Beaubien glances in her direction. "I have visits to make before I leave town, both to the jail and to Ignacia Jaramillo in preparation for the governor's visit next week." He rises from his seat. "Perhaps we can speak more about this issue while he is here."

"Ah yes. Charles Bent is the other silent partner in your land grant endeavor, isn't he?" Gerald gets to his feet and nods to Alma and Andrew. "Consider it done."

CHAPTER 16 – JANUARY 9, 1847
Taos, New Mexico

Governor Bent still hasn't reached Taos the following Saturday, although Tomás Romero has, back from a snowy trip to Santa Fe. He arrives at the Peabody house accompanied by a short, thin, old Spanish man with a weathered face, sharp eyes, and thin lips who Jeremiah greets politely.

"Señor Montoya," he says as they come in, then they're both distracted by Romero, who is settling himself into the cushioned chair closest to the fire with a deep sigh. Romero grins at Jeremiah. "My bones tell me I must begin to allow more time to recover from midwinter journeys."

Jeremiah waves Montoya to a seat and drops into the chair opposite. "My own bones tell me this is not a usual winter," he says. "The snow remains on the ground even here in Taos. Usually it has melted by the end of the third day."

Romero nods. "The journey from Santa Fe was a difficult one. The snow was up to the horses' knees in some places. The next storm will block the road completely." Then he shrugs and turns to Alma and her father, his eyes twinkling. "But your valley is cut off every winter, is it not?"

Montoya swings his head, looking at them sharply.

Andrew comes in with an armload of firewood. He nods to the others and moves to the fireplace as Gerald says, "It's true. Palo Flechado Pass is easily blocked. Once snow falls in that valley, it tends to stay on the ground until spring."

"And then turns the ground into a mess of mud," Andrew says as he crouches down to stack the wood against the adobe wall. He sits back on his heels and smiles at Romero. "Welcome back, señor. How was Santa Fe?"

"It smelled of los soldados americanos," the Taos Pueblo man says gravely.

Alma suppresses a laugh and even Montoya's thin lips quirk in amusement. Romero turns to Jeremiah. "There has been much sickness." He spreads his hands and looks down at them. "I pray I have not carried it back to my people."

Gerald frowns. "Sickness? Of what kind?"

"The spotted disease you call measles. And a disease of the belly. The thing the americano doctors say is flux." He shrugs. "However, illnesses of the body are not the greatest trouble of those who lead los americanos."

"I pray they have much trouble," Montoya says in a low, savage voice.

Andrew has crossed the room now and taken a seat beside Alma, on the cushioned bench next to the bookcase. He frowns at Romero. "The American soldiers are unhappy?"

The Taos leader smiles at him. "I am told they are discouraged and wish only to return to their homes." He shoots a quick glance at the other men. "They are without discipline and spend much time in drinking establishments and gambling halls." His eyes twinkle as he turns to Jeremiah. "The officers call the rooms for monte and other games of chance 'dens of iniquity.'"

Jeremiah Peabody smiles. "While I tend to agree with them, those so-called gambling dens undoubtedly contain persons with whom the American military leaders would do well to acquaint themselves."

"Los ricos," Montoya says bitterly. "Those who know nothing of us."

Romero grins wryly. "The rich ones of Santa Fe," he agrees. Then he sobers. "It is possible the recent discovery of the plot against los americanos took place in those rooms."

Alma, watching Señor Montoya, sees a look of pure fury cross his face. "Betrayed by a priest, no doubt," he mutters, but the other men don't seem to hear him.

"It's likely the plotting itself occurred there," her grandfather agrees. "It might very well have succeeded if Charles Bent hadn't had friends in those so-called dens."

"That Bent!" Montoya growls.

There's a long pause, then Gerald says, "Santa Fe has always been a hotbed of intrigue. If the rebels really wanted to succeed, they would do well to organize themselves outside of Santa Fe."

"As we did in thirty-seven," Montoya says. "Our mistake then was to try to take that city of priests and politicians."

Gerald looks at him. "You were a leader in that fight?"

"I was. I would not make the same error twice."

Gerald and Jeremiah study him, but Montoya falls silent, his lips a thin line above his proud chin.

"Many good men died in that final set of battles with Governor Armijo's troops," Jeremiah says gravely.

Gerald glances at Alma, whose shoulders are suddenly tense with memory, then Andrew, who is studying the floor. "My wife and children were in Santa Fe during that insurrection," he says quietly. "It was a terrible time."

The old man's head jerks. "It will be another terrible time if los americanos do not respect us and our traditions," he growls. Then he shrugs. "At least this time el padre supports our cause."

"Padre Martínez?" Gerald turns toward him. "What do you mean?"

The other man grins, a wolfish look in his eyes. "The padre understands what will happen to his own authority, now that los soldados americanos have arrived. How they will support Bent and not him. He speaks freely of the need to resist them and protect las tradiciones." Montoya pauses, studying his listeners. "He also reminds us that the war, it has not yet ended. Mexico has not surrendered the fight."

Jeremiah frowns. "The padre would do well to minimize such talk. It has the potential to rile people into futile rebellion."

"Perhaps not so futile. Mexico City has not surrendered to los americanos."

Romero studies the fire. "Resistance must be sudden and strong, and must rise in the north," he says. "Where the snow is so deep that the wagons of the americano cannon cannot travel through it."

"The walls of our houses are thick and strong," Montoya says.

Gerald lifts an eyebrow at Romero. "Why do you speak of cannon?"

"A leader of the December conspiracy fled to Albuquerque, where he hid in an old building," the pueblo leader says. "It was, of course, made of adobe brick, although long untended. Much of the plaster had worn away, exposing the inner core. When the man refused to come out, los americanos brought a cannon."

Andrew frowns. "A cannon against one man?"

"Los soldados americanos, they are careless of many things," Montoya tells him. "Including the amount of gunpowder they expend."

Jeremiah has been staring thoughtfully at the fire. Now he stirs. "How did the adobe hold up?"

"I was told the walls sustained a good deal of damage without giving way. The man who told me said the cannon's smoke drove the rebel out, not its shells."

"Interesting." Alma's grandfather studies him, then Montoya. "I hope you do not plan to test the power of those cannon here in Taos."

Romero's eyes glint with an amusement that gives nothing away. "The snow is very deep. By the time cannon arrive from Santa Fe, we will have news from ciudad de México that the war, it is finished."

Jeremiah gazes at him, his high forehead furrowed with concern. "I know you are a careful man, Tomás, and consider all aspects of a situation before you address it."

Romero's eyes twinkle at him. "And so?" He rises from his seat. Montoya follows.

Jeremiah frowns and pushes himself from his chair. "I hope others who are of your way of thinking will also carefully evaluate their choices and the possible consequences that might result from any action they choose to take."

Gerald nods. "It is natural to want to resist," he says mildly. "The question is whether it is wise."

As the men exchange the usual farewell rituals, Romero pats Gerald's shoulder. "Your speech is as enigmatic as that of my people," he says teasingly. "Perhaps we should ask you to join us."

The American men smile thinly as Montoya snorts in disgust and moves toward the door.

TERESINA

CHAPTER 17 – JANUARY 18, 1847
Taos, New Mexico

It snowed every day of the week before Father arrived. I was on tenterhooks, going to the gate as often as I could find a reason to be in the courtyard, drooping with disappointment when the street remained empty of everything but the occasional passerby hurrying to get out of the falling white flakes.

On Sunday during Mass, I said a special prayer asking for him to arrive soon and for a safe journey. Mother had become doubtful he would come at all. "The road along the river is dangerously icy this time of year," she pointed out. "And the mountain route will be difficult for the horses."

But still I hoped. Rumalda and Tía Josefa did their best to distract me through that long afternoon, and on the next evening set me to learning to make tortillas. I had just achieved my first relatively round one when there was a sudden commotion in the courtyard.

"He's here!" Alfredo cried. He and Estefina rushed outside as Rumalda put her hand on my shoulder, keeping me in place so I wouldn't spread wet corn flour across the room.

Mother was in the big chair by the fire, sewing a new shirt for my father. She looked at the door, then me, and shook her head. "You three are going to wear out those hinges," she said.

Estefina came back in. "But it truly is Papa!"

Mother dropped her work and went with her into the court-yard. Rumalda handed me a cloth, and I hurriedly wiped my hands and followed.

There he was, oblivious to the falling snow as he hugged my brother and sister and beamed at my mother as if he'd never seen her before. When he saw me, his tired face brightened even more. He released Alfredo and Estefina, crouched down and opened his arms. "And here is our Teresina!"

I ran across the courtyard, the snow swirling against my cheeks. "Father! You came!"

"Of course I came, pequeña. Did you think I would never come back?"

I tucked my face into his shoulder. "You didn't come for Christmas."

He squeezed me to his chest, then released me. "I'm here now." He stood up and reached for my mother's hand, then turned toward the gate, where a group of men stood watching. They included my godfather, Cornelio Vigil, and also my mother's brother, Uncle Pablo.

Tío Pablo had his hand on the arm of a slender young man with creamy skin, dark hair, and amused eyes. "Children, do you remember Don Narciso?" he asked.

We exchanged glances and slowly shook our heads, then Alfredo brightened. "The Narciso of Don Carlos?" he asked. "The one who is returning from la universidad?"

"The Narciso of Señorita Luz," Estefina said.

The newcomer smiled at her. "I am glad to know my sister has not forgotten me."

"She talks about you all the time!" I blurted. Everyone turned to look at me, and I tucked myself into my mother's skirts.

There was another man behind Narciso and Tío Pablo. My father gestured him forward and turned to my mother. "My dear," he said. "Allow me to introduce our new Prosecuting Attorney for northern New Mexico, James White Leal. Mr. Leal, my wife, Doña Maria Ignacia."

Mr. Leal took off his hat and swept her a low bow. "Mrs. Bent." He was a pretty man with blue eyes and curly brown shoulder length hair highlighted by the snow. He brushed the flakes away from his face and turned his eyes toward my half sister and aunt. As my father introduced them, I saw the way he looked at them and tucked myself further against my mother. There was something in his gaze I didn't like. At the time, I thought he was a little rude. Now I know his look was supercilious. As if he had already tried us all and found us wanting.

My mother must have sensed my discomfort. She nudged me toward the house. "Children, go ask Guadalupe to prepare hot chocolate."

"And tortillas!" I turned to my father. "I learned to make tortillas today!"

He laughed and glanced at Rumalda. "With a little help, perhaps?"

"Just a little," she said. "Welcome home, Papa."

He smiled at her. "Thank you, my dear. And how is your new husband?"

"I'm afraid he's stuck at Bent's Fort," she said ruefully as they followed us into the house.

Don Narciso was anxious to see his mother and sisters, so he and Tío Pablo only remained long enough to admire my tortilla-making skills before they ventured back out into the snow. My godfather followed them a few minutes later, taking Mr. Leal with him.

My mother set about dishing up leftover stew as Guadalupe made additional tortillas and my father stripped off his wet outer garments. "This new attorney of prosecution appears to be a most unsympathetic person," Mama said as she reached for another bowl.

"Though very good looking," Estefina said. She was standing by Father's chair, proffering a dry pair of socks. "He has a fine, strong face, a long straight nose, and beautiful hair."

"Ah, just what I wished for," Father said, taking the socks. He looked up at my mother. "Leal's whip smart and eager to prove himself. And he seems to know the law. I think he'll be helpful in the effort to get the people here to see reason."

"Americano law," Guadalupe muttered.

He grinned at her. "Yes, americano law. The one we're living under now." He looked at my mother. "I expect Leal will help set that calf Padre Martínez back a peg or two."

"It will only give him more to complain about."

Father's eyes narrowed. "I'll put him in jail for contempt and sedition, if he's not careful."

He'd finished his meal and my mother, aunt, and half sister were bringing him up to date on the local news when there was a knock at the gate. Alfredo went to answer it and came back saying men from Taos pueblo wanted to speak with el gobernador and had asked that he meet them at the jail across the broad street from the house.

Father lifted me from his knee. "No rest for the wicked," he grumbled, but I could see he was pleased.

When he returned an hour later, Estefina and I were drowsing on the little bench carved into the adobe wall near the fireplace, pretending to be asleep so Mother wouldn't send us to bed. I squinted my eyes just enough to see without attracting her attention and watched my parents.

Father's good humor had disappeared, replaced by irritation. When he took off his hat, his hair was limp with damp snow. Mother rushed to find a linen towel.

"Stupidity and recalcitrance!" he exclaimed as he rubbed it on his head.

"The girls are sleeping," Mother said softly and he dropped his voice, but I could still hear him.

"Luis Lee brought in some pueblo men in late December and Cornelio Vigil found evidence they'd stolen at least three fanegas of corn — that's over ten bushels — from one of the outlying haciendas. So he put them in jail, where they ought to be. Tomás Romero and his friends dragged me away from you this evening to give me a lecture about how the culprits need to be home to care for their families and Romero will stand bond."

Father gave his hair one more hard rub, then tossed the towel aside and sat down in his chair. "He can't seem to understand that things are different now. Those men have been remanded to court, and they'll stay in jail until the next session."

"When will that be?" she asked.

"April, or so Leal told me on the way up here." He ran his hands through his hair, straightening it. "Maybe by then the prisoners will have decided to confess what they've done and explain how they plan to make reparations. Even if I had the legal authority to release them, I wouldn't. They all need a good

lesson in the American rule of law, and that's what I told Romero." He sniffed. "I made sure the rest of them heard, as well. There were entirely too many people milling around that jail. I'm going to talk to the sheriff tomorrow about establishing a curfew for the entire valley." He grinned. "I told Romero that, too. You should have seen the look on his face. The horror!" He tilted his head back and laughed out loud.

"Hush!" Mother said. "You'll wake las niñas!"

He paused and turned to study us. I closed my eyes just in time.

"Shouldn't they be in their beds?"

"It's been a long and eventful day. I didn't have the heart to disturb them."

"Ummm." He must have reached for her hand and drawn her into his lap, because I heard a slight gasp and small laugh. "You're still wet," she said, but there was a smile in her voice.

"You can dry me off in the bedroom," he said, and she laughed again. "You go on," she said. "Just let me bank the fire."

As he moved toward the blanket-covered doorway to their room, I snuggled closer to Estefina. Father was home. I was content.

ALMA

CHAPTER 18 – EARLY JANUARY 19, 1847
Taos, New Mexico

Alma jerks awake to the sound of a fist banging on wood planks. She frowns, confused, then realizes the noise is coming from the door to the courtyard. There's another thud, then voices. Anamaria's, shrill with anger and fear. A lower male sound, placating. Her response, louder this time. Then closer. "¡Señores!" she cries. "¡Señores!"

Alma grabs her green-and-yellow shawl and throws it over her head as she dashes into the hall. Her grandfather stands at his door, holding a candle. The shadows it casts emphasize the terror in Anamaria's face, the sullen look in Juan Pacheco's, who is behind her.

"It's all right," he says.

"You know nothing!" she snaps over her shoulder, then swings toward Jeremiah Peabody. "The sheriff is dead." She glances at Juan. "And el prefecto also?"

When he nods, Jeremiah's candle swings wildly. He braces his arm against the adobe wall. "Lee? And Vigil, too?"

Alma's father and brother appear behind him. "What's hap-pened?" Gerald demands.

"Luis Lee and Cornelio Vigil are both dead." Jeremiah straightens and looks beyond Anamaria to her son. "What happened?"

"When?" Gerald asks.

Jeremiah's candle wobbles again and Alma slips toward him and takes it. "Let's go into the parlor," she suggests. Then she glances at Anamaria. "Or the kitchen?"

The housekeeper nods, and they all follow her and settle themselves around the table. The fire has been lit and the big pottery mixing bowl is on the counter. The window shutter is half open. Snow edges the ledge.

Gerald turns to Juan Pacheco. "What happened?"

"And why were you there?" Anamaria demands.

"Please, Mama. Let me explain."

She scowls at him, then subsides. Her work-worn hands dab at the tabletop as if searching for crumbs. Alma reaches for her, but she jerks away. "Speak!" she snaps at her son.

Juan spreads his hands, palms up. He clicks his tongue. "I was at the jail yesterday night, speaking with the men who Luis Lee imprisoned for a mere fanega of corn."

"Those men from the pueblo?" Gerald asks.

"I believe they stole more than one fanega," Jeremiah says. "Two and a half bushels wouldn't be worth putting them in jail."

Juan shakes his head impatiently. "Whatever the amount, it wasn't necessary to lock them away until the court session in April. They have families to feed. When word got out that Bent is here—"

"Charles has returned?"

Juan nods. "We sent for him." He looks at his mother. "Or rather, Tomás Romero did." His voice changes, becomes low and bitter. "Bent came and said he could do nothing. The law is different now. The accused men must remain in jail all the winter instead of providing sustenance for their families." He scowls. "Then Bent went off to his warm bed and Ignacia and her brood. And the warm solicitations of the Beaubiens, as well, no doubt, since he carted their precious Narciso with him from Santa Fe."

Andrew sits up. "Narciso is back?"

Gerald grins at him, then sobers as he turns back to Pacheco. "And then?"

"Then Luis Lee and Tomás Romero talked some more, and Pablo Montoya came in and there was more talk, and then Lee said, está bien, he would release the men on Romero's recogni—" He stumbles a little on the word and Jeremiah nods.

"Recognizance, yes. That is the procedure used under Mexican law."

"But not American." Juan's voice grows bitter again. "And not Governor Bent's or Cornelio Vigil's." His lips twist. "Not that Vigil's opinion matters much anymore." He looks at Jeremiah. "The prefect came in while Lee was unlocking the door and started shouting that the law must be obeyed, and he wouldn't allow—."

Anamaria is staring at him, her hand over her mouth. He clicks his tongue. "If he'd stayed away, he'd still be alive, not lying on the floor of the jail with a knife—" Alma shudders involuntarily and he stops abruptly. "Pardon, señorita." He looks at his mother. "Mama."

"So Lee was about to release the prisoners, Vigil intervened, and they were both killed," Gerald says.

Pacheco nods. "Vigil there in the jail. Lee ran out and made it to his house, but we—" He glances at his mother. "They chased him down the street and to his house." He grimaces. "Lee ran inside, then reappeared on the roof with a rifle and started shooting."

Alma's grandfather moves restlessly in his seat. Juan nods at him. "That really set them off. Someone threw a hatchet and then the arrows started flying." He lays his hands on the table and studies them. "He didn't last long."

Jeremiah lifts his head. "Do you know for a fact that he's dead?"

"There were a great many arrows."

Gerald leans forward. "You keep saying 'they.' Who did all this?"

Juan glances at his mother again. "People from the pueblo. People from here." He shrugs and clicks his tongue. "Pablo Montoya. Tomás Romero."

Alma feels the breath leave her body. Señor Romero?

But then Juan shrugs again. "That is, Romero was there at the beginning, at the jail. I don't know about later, at the casa of Señor Lee."

"And where are they now?" Alma's father asks. "This— group?"

Juan shrugs. "Roaming around. There was some talk about Beaubien and the other Americans."

"Carlos Beaubien isn't American," Andrew says. "He's French. Well, French Canadian."

"And he's not in Taos right now, anyway," Gerald says. "He left yesterday for Tierra Amarilla."

Juan shrugs again and looks at his hands. "That's all I know."

Andrew sits back, his brow furrowed. "Narcisco is there, though. In a house full of women." He turns to his father.

"It's still dark out," Gerald says. "Wait until morning."

Andrew crosses his arms. His chin jerks in what looks like acquiescence, but he doesn't meet anyone's eyes. Alma opens her mouth to second her father's statement but then shuts it again. If Josefa or Rumalda were in a similar situation, she'd want to go to them.

Anamaria leans forward. "And the Bent casa? Will this mob go there as well?"

Her son glances at her, clicks his tongue, and looks back down at his hands. "Anything is possible."

Her lips tighten. "Idiots, all of you. This isn't the way or the time."

"You are a woman."

She pushes back from the table. The braid coiled on the top of her head shakes with indignation. "And you are a fool. Get out of my kitchen."

He looks around the room, taking in Jeremiah Peabody's pale face and upright form, Gerald's square forehead, Andrew's brown skin and blond hair, and Alma's wild black curls. Juan's mouth twists. He rises from his seat. "You have made your allegiances plain," he tells his mother. "May you suffer for it." He brushes past her toward the outer door.

The kitchen fills with silence. A long moment, then Anamaria huffs and turns toward the stove. "A fool and an idiot," she mutters under her breath. She grabs the poker and adjusts the fire, then turns toward the table. "He was always a tempestuous one and given to exaggeration." She points the poker at the empty door to the hall. "Es probable que no one has been killed, and the mob has worn off their excitement and gone home to their beds."

"And Lee is tucked safe inside his house with an arrow in his arm that will give him a story to tell," Gerald says.

But Andrew doesn't participate in the general chuckle of agreement, and when the others head back to their rooms to rest until daylight, he slips out the door to the courtyard.

At the other end of the hall, Gerald turns at the sound of the door. "Where is he going at this hour?"

Alma shrugs. "The outhouse?"

Her father frowns, studying the heavy wooden planks, then huffs slightly and moves toward his room. Alma slips into her own, lies down on the bed, and waits for dawn.

TERESINA

CHAPTER 19 – EARLY JANUARY 19, 1847
Taos, New Mexico

My recollections of that morning are tinged with red.

Though my first impression was of noise. Scrabbling sounds on the flat, dirt-topped roof above my head. Shouting in the courtyard.

I moved Estefina's arm from my chest and struggled upright. Guadalupe was at the wood-plank door. She'd opened it just enough to peer out into the gray dimness of early dawn. "¿Qué es?" she asked roughly.

"¡El gobernador!" a man shouted.

I rubbed the sleep from my eyes.

"You're drunk!" Guadalupe said. "You come back." She put her shoulder to the door, to shove it closed, and someone on the other side pushed back. "Go away!" she shouted, forgetting that the rest of us were supposed to be sleeping.

"Lupe?" my father asked from the blanket-covered opening to the other room. "What is it?" He tucked in his shirt as he came in, his suspenders still dangling from the top of his trousers.

She heaved at the door, closing the gap, and slid the bolt back into place, then turned and scowled at him. "Borrachos," she sniffed. "Drunks. I tell them go away."

He grinned at her, but then someone outside began pounding on the boards. I could hear chanting, too. And a drum?

Father's face changed. He pulled his suspenders up over his shoulders and moved to the door.

Guadalupe went to the fire and the bowl of masa she'd been mixing for the morning tortillas. Beside me, Estefina sat up and rubbed her eyes. "What's that noise?" she asked.

"People to see father."

There was a thud overhead. She squinted up at the latillas. "Is there someone on the roof?"

I shrugged. Father was at the door now. He shifted the bolt and opened the door just enough to see out. "What do you want?" he asked.

Estefina craned her head to see beyond him. "The snow has stopped," she said as someone yelled "¡Tu cabeza!!"

She pulled back, eyes big, head flat against the adobe wall.

At the door, my father let out an exasperated sigh. "Why would you want my head?" he asked. "I've always helped you when I was able, seen that justice was done."

"¡No más gobernadores!" someone shouted.

Father snorted impatiently. "No more governors? You will always have someone to rule over you."

"Not anglos!"

A chant went up. "No anglo rule! No anglo rule!" Then it changed. "Kill the anglos! Kill the anglos!"

Father laughed again, but there was anxiety in his tone now. I reached for Estefina's hand. Mother appeared in the doorway to their room. "What is it?" she asked.

"Get back!" Father barked at the crowd. Mother rushed toward him. I heard a thud, then another one, and an arrow flew past his head toward the fireplace. As another one followed, he ducked out of the way and put both hands on the door, shoving it closed as Mother helped. She reached for the bolt and pushed it into place.

They turned to face the room, backs against the door. Then my mother jerked in surprise and grabbed her left side. "¡Ay!" she said.

He pulled her toward the table as Guadalupe dropped what she was doing and hurried toward them.

Father looked back at the door. An arrowhead protruded from the planks. It had struck Mother in the side. "I think it's just a scratch," he told Guadalupe as he released Mother into her care. But his face was angry now.

An axe slammed into the door, splintering the planks. Firelight glinted on its sharp edge, then someone on the other side wrenched it free, leaving a gap. Fists slammed into the boards. And something bigger. A block of firewood?

Somewhere there was a high keening, a thin high wail that went on an on. Then Estefina slapped me and it stopped. I caught my breath and saw blood running down Father's forehead.

Josefa and Rumalda appeared in the room simultaneously, Alfredo behind them. Josefa went to my mother and Rumalda to my father, each reaching to staunch the bleeding. Father shook Rumalda off. "Go!" he said.

"Where?" she asked.

Josefa moved away from Mother, snatched the poker from the fire and grabbed a metal stirring spoon from Guadalupe's mixing bowl. She gestured toward my parent's room. "The back wall," she said. "Into the Lashone's house."

My mother stared at her for a long minute. The Lashones weren't home. They'd been gone all winter, on a trading trip into the northern mountains. Josefa moved impatiently and Mama nodded, then turned to Estefina and me, shooing us with her hands. "Go," she said. "Quickly! Go with her!"

"You're hurt," I whimpered.

"Not badly. Go!"

The blows on the door had increased by then. The boards screeched as they splintered. An arrow flew through the widening cracks, hit Father in the cheek, and cut into his chin.

"Papa!" Estefina yelled, but my mother shouted "Go!" again and ran toward us. As she pulled us off the adobe bench, Father cried out. Another arrow had pierced his skin, this one across his forehead.

Alfredo dashed across the room to Father's office. A minute later, he returned with the shotgun. "Into the back!" Mother yelled, but he rushed toward Father instead, holding out the gun. As arrows poured into the room, Father shook his head.

"Please!" Alfredo begged. "Let me!"

Father took the gun. "Go with your mother," he said.

Overhead, the ceiling latillas began to crack. Dirt rained into the room. Father lifted his head. "Stop!" he bellowed at it. He turned toward the door, where the muzzle of a rifle had appeared, moving from side to side as if it could see where we were. "Stop!" he yelled again.

The gun roared. The bullet zinged past him and into a pan by the fire. Father turned wildly. Another shot blasted into the room.

"Children! Come!" Mother shouted. She grabbed Alfredo's arm and shoved at Estefana, then reached for me, pulling us toward the door to the back.

I looked over my shoulder at Father and saw him grab his side and double over in pain. "Go!" he yelled at me. "Go!" Then he swung toward Guadalupe, who still stood by the fireplace, holding her bowl of masa, her eyes wide with shock. "Go!" he yelled again.

In the other room, Rumalda was jabbing at the wall with the fire poker, breaking off small pieces of adobe while Josefa scraped it away with the big spoon. Guadalupe rushed past me and Estefina and pushed Rumalda aside.

"Like this!" she said, grabbing the poker. She held it like a spear and rammed it deep into the sunbaked brick, then yanked it back and forth like a lever. "Help me!" she gasped. She moved closer to the wall, making room for Rumalda's hands on the far end, and together they exerted more pressure on the brick.

A large chunk popped out and Josefa kicked it out of the way. "Again!" she cried.

My mother had disappeared into the front room. She came back now, carrying Father's pistols. She laid them on the floor and pulled a leather box from under the bed, the container Father used for extra ammunition.

"Mama?" Estefina asked. "What are—"

"Hush!" Mama snapped, lifting the nearest gun. "My hands are shaking! Alfredo, help me!" He hurried to her.

They had just finished loading the guns when Josefa exclaimed, "We did it!"

Rumalda turned toward my sister and me. "Estefina, you first," she said. "Let's see if you fit."

I hung back, eyes on my mother, who moved toward the front room with a loaded pistol in each hand.

"Ignacia!" Josefa cried, but Mama was already gone.

"She's through!" Rumalda said from the hole in the wall. "Alfredo! Teresina! Come!"

But I had crept to the door to the other room and hidden behind the blanket to watch my parents.

There were big gaps in the outer door now, more arrows on the floor, and another in my father's body. This one was in his left shoulder, driven straight in from the side. The shotgun lay near the table. Mother kicked it aside as she offered him the pistols, but he shook his head.

"Then go!" she shouted. "There are horses in the corral! Go!"

"I am governor!" he yelled back at her. "I will not flee!" He looked toward the door. "What would they do to you if I did?"

She dropped the pistols beside the shotgun and grabbed his arm. "We have a way out! Come!"

I backed away from the door as they entered. Rumalda was bent over the hole, talking to Estefina on the other side. "No!" she said. "Stay there! I'll find her!"

Mother led Father across the room. "You see?" she said, pointing at the hole.

"Teresina!" Tía Josefa said. "Come, child!"

My parents turned toward me, and I ran into my father's arms. My face bumped his chin and he pulled back, wincing. "Father!" I cried.

He lifted me into the hole in the adobe wall. "Go, child." Then he stood back and gestured to my aunt and half-sister, but they had turned toward the bed, where Guadalupe was stripping off blankets.

"What are you doing?" my mother cried to her. "Come!"

"They'll take them all!" Guadalupe said. "Help me!"

As Mother shook her head and went toward her, there was a tremendous crash in the outer room.

"The door has fallen!" Father cried. "Hurry!" He turned to me. "Go on!" I eased further into the hole, looking backward, then stopped, frozen by what I saw.

A hand grabbed at the door blanket and threw it to the floor. A man appeared, holding Father's pistols. He pointed them at my father, then Mother, who rushed toward him. As he cocked it, Guadalupe dashed into the gap between, her arms full of blankets. The gun roared and she crumpled to the floor. She didn't seem to have any face.

"You bastard!" Mama cried. She hurried to Guadalupe and crouched over her.

The man swung the gun, butt first, into her back. "She's just a slave!" he growled. "You don't care about her!"

Mama looked up, her face streaked with tears. "You know nothing!"

"Ignacia!" Father yelled. There was real desperation in his voice now. He swung to face the man with the pistols. "She's a woman of your own people! Don't hurt her!"

"Go!" Mother yelled at him. "Go!"

"Come!"

She looked up at the man with the gun, then at Father. "They want to kill you, not me! Go! Hurry!"

He scowled but obeyed. I scrambled into the room ahead of him, then turned back to watch. He ducked into the hole, but the arrow in his shoulder jutted out, blocking his way. He snapped the fletch off impatiently, then reached for the one in his cheek. This was made of stronger stuff. It merely twisted, angling away from the front of his face. But it wasn't jutting sideways any-more. The shaft of the one in his shoulder scraped the adobe as he came through, bringing a trickle of dirt into the room.

"Get me a pencil!" Father gasped at Rumalda as he col-lapsed onto the floor. "And something to write on."

She ran around the room wildly, looking for what he wanted, as Josefa helped my mother into the room. "Here," Mother said, fumbling at her skirt. "Use my memoranda book."

"I found a pencil," Rumalda gasped as she took the little book. She knelt to lift Father's head into her lap so he could write.

Mama crouched beside me and my siblings. "Are you all right?"

"Why won't he fight, Mama?" Tears ran down Alfredo's face. "I want to fight!"

And then Tomás Romero came through the wall. Josefa swung at him with the poker, but he brushed her aside. He and his bow and arrows seemed to fill the space between the ceiling and my father. His face was a mask of rage. Father looked up at him with a grimace of disgust. "Romero?" he asked. "I thought you had more sense."

Romero dropped his bow, bent down, and grabbed my father by his suspenders, lifting him into the air. "You!" he bellowed. "If you had listened to reason, none of this would have hap-pened!" And then he dropped him to the floor with a thud as Rumalda shrieked and scrambled out of the way.

Father's eyes rolled in their sockets. "¡Mi amor!" Mama cried, but before she could get to him, Romero seized his bow and drew its string across the base of my father's scalp. When he straightened, there was a tangle of black hair in his hand and the top of Father's head was a mass of blood.

Estefina shrieked and I screamed and Alfredo bellowed and surged forward, but Tía Josefa pulled him back. Mama rushed to our father as Romero turned away. The ceiling above us cracked open then, and the room was suddenly full of people: men and women with wild faces, some from above, some from the hole in the wall. Oddly, the door on the far side that led to the Lashone's courtyard remained closed. Old man Lashone must have barricaded his gate very strongly.

People crowded the room, looming over us. I clutched at my brother and sister as Josefa muttered inarticulate prayers.

Then Mother cried "My darling!" again and I knew from her voice that my father was dead.

ALMA

CHAPTER 20 – JANUARY 19, 1847
Taos, New Mexico

Alma has drifted into an uneasy sleep when she suddenly hears voices outside her door. Her father and— Anamaria? Alma pushes her hair away from her face and slips across the room and into the hall.

Her grandfather is there, too. Still in his nightshirt, his face gaunt in the pale light drifting from the open door to the court-yard. Snow covers the ground outside.

Anamaria's hair is down in a thick waist-length braid and her eyes are wide with fear. "My son returned por un momento," she says. "El gobernador is dead."

Gerald squints at her. "Bent? That mob from the jail got him, too?"

The housekeeper nods, her lips working. "And Doña Josefa's older brother, that Pablo." She glances toward Alma. "And the Beaubien boy."

Alma's heart stills as her grandfather sways and reaches for the nearest wall. Her father turns toward Andrew's room. "Andrew?" he calls. "Son?" But his voice is bleak. He already knows the answer to his question. Andrew isn't there.

"Come," Jeremiah Peabody says. He is once again firmly on his feet, his old head tall on his shoulders. "We'll find him." He turns toward his room, then looks back. "Rifle," he tells Alma.

Her father, already heading down the hall, turns his head. "And the shotgun," he adds.

Alma nods and hurries off, glad to have something to occupy her hands, at least. She has the guns and ammunition ready when the men emerge. Her father reaches for the shotgun, and her grandfather takes the rifle. Then he stops and stares down at it for a long minute. He turns and leans the gun against the wall.

"Sir?" Gerald asks.

Jeremiah shakes his head. "I have never carried a gun against my neighbors in this town and I won't begin now."

"There's a mob out there," Gerald says. "They're not thinking right. It's more like carrying protection against wild dogs."

Jeremiah closes his eyes, opens them. "I cannot."

Gerald stands staring at him, then steps around him to place the shotgun beside the rifle. He turns to Alma and Anamaria, who's emerged from the kitchen with a cup of coffee in each hand. "Do not hesitate to use them," he says flatly.

Surely it won't come to that. But there's something in his face that keeps Alma from saying so. She nods mutely. Anamaria proffers the coffee and the men quaff the hot liquid, nod their thanks, and head out the door and across the courtyard.

As he lifts the bar from the gate, Jeremiah turns and gestures to the women. "Shut this behind us!" he calls.

Then they are gone. Anamaria crosses to the gate, closes it up tight, and stands for a long minute, her head bowed. Then she crosses herself and returns to Alma, who's watching from the door.

Now all they can do is wait. The sun rises and moves into the sky, and still the streets are silent. Perhaps it was all a bad dream. At some point, Anamaria puts her hair up, makes fresh tortillas, and brings out creamy newly made goat cheese, but Alma's throat is too dry to swallow.

The sun moves across the blue sky. There are no shadows in the snowy walled courtyard. Alma goes out to retrieve wood for the fire and stands listening. Are those voices? Shouts from the direction of the plaza? Or is her imagination playing tricks? Her breath catches and there's a sharp pain in her belly. Where are her father and grandfather? And Andrew?

And then another shout. This one is definitely in the street, toward the direction of the plaza. Anamaria appears at the house door. She hears it, too. A strand of hair has come out of her braided crown. She moves past Alma to the gate and slides the little shutter over the square gate peephole to one side. Alma places her armload of firewood on the chopping stump and goes to stand beside her and look out.

There's no one in the street. "Where are they?" the girl mutters. Anamaria shakes her head. The snow on the street is still unmarked except for the footprints of the two men hours earlier. They've softened a little around the edges. Alma shivers.

"You should go inside," Anamaria says.

"I'm not cold."

Something moves near the plaza. She stretches to see more clearly and the housekeeper sucks in a breath, then says, "Not los señores. These have weapons."

A group of men and boys appear, churning the snow into mud. Most of them carry bows and arrows but a few have guns, and at least two have axes over their shoulders. Anamaria pulls back, slaps the little shutter into place, latches it, and hurries toward the house. Alma frowns and moves the board cautiously, just enough to see out. The men have been joined by a handful of women. Alma doesn't recognize any of them.

As the crowd gets closer to the Peabody casa, Anamaria returns with the shotgun and a rebozo. She leans the gun against the gate and hands the long shawl to Alma. "Put it on," she says. "Cover your hair."

Alma steps back and begins wrapping herself up. Anamaria moves to the peephole. She peers out, mutters a low oath, then jerks back.

"What is it?" Alma asks.

"The señor and your father," the housekeeper says. She moves aside just enough to allow Alma to see. They peer into the street.

The two men are moving up the street toward the Peabody gate. The mob has broken into two groups, one closer to the house and one hanging back in the direction of the plaza. As Alma's father and grandfather pass this cluster, someone makes a jeering comment. Gerald's head jerks toward them, but Jeremiah touches his elbow and they continue steadily toward the casa.

Then the group between them and the gate moves in front of them, blocking the way. "What are you doing, old man?" a voice yells.

"I'm going home," Jeremiah says calmly. "What are you doing?"

"Hunting for gringos!" someone else yells. "Americano scum who think they're better than us!"

Air whistles between Anamaria's teeth and she shakes her head. "Fools and idiots," she mutters.

Then there's a shout from the plaza end of the street. More people arrive, men and women alike. "Everything's gone from the Bent house!" one of them yells.

"We wiped it clean!" a man shouts. "No more filthy americanos ruling us!"

And then they surge toward the two Americans, now caught between the two groups. Alma reaches for the crossbar that holds the gate shut, but Anamaria grabs her arm, forcing it away. "Didn't you hear that?" she hisses. "They'll be trying to get in here, next!"

"But Papa!"

There's a shout in the street and a kind of low, animal-like growl. Alma peers out. She can't see her father or her grandfather. Just the people in the crowd, who have their backs to her.

A man turns to stare at the gate. There's a jagged scar on his cheek. The man from the pueblo on Christmas Day? Then he swings back to the crowd. It seems to be circling around something in its center. Her father and grandfather? There in the mud? Oh, God.

She spots Manuel Paiz at the edge of the crowd, his brother Ysidro behind him. Manuel casts an anxious look toward the Peabody gate and begins to shove forward into the crowd, but his brother pulls him back.

Somewhere in the middle of the milling group, an axe swings upward, its sharpened edge bright in the winter sunlight.

"¡Dios!" Anamaria gasps.

The crowd shifts and falls back. Alma's grandfather is crumpled in a lanky heap, his back to the gate. Her father sprawls beside him on his stomach, his head turned her direction, his gray eyes empty of life.

"Papa!" she howls. Faces turn toward the gate, then Anamaria is yanking her away and someone is screaming. The mob moves toward the house.

Anamaria reaches past Alma, slams the little wooden shutter closed, and grips the girl's arms hard enough to hurt. "¡Silencio!" she growls in Alma's ear. "¡Silencio!"

"Papa," Alma gasps. "And Grandfather, too! Oh, God!"

The housekeeper's face is grim as she nods. On the other side of the gate, a fist slams against its tall planks. "¡Abre la puerta!" voices howl. "Open the gate!"

Anamaria's face darkens. She reaches for the shotgun. "They may be my relatives, but this is my home." She gestures for Alma to open the little aperture in the gate, then sticks the tip of the shotgun barrel through it. She can't really see where it's pointing, but she yells, "¡Dispararé!" anyway. "I'll shoot!" she bellows again. "Get away!"

An arrow flies at the gate and bites into the board beside the peephole. "Bastards!" Anamaria howls. She pulls at the shotgun, cocking it. "Get away!"

Alma moves to one side, so she can see past the shotgun barrel and into the street toward the plaza. A man in a broad-brimmed leather hat appears, waving his arms. "What are you doing?" he yells at the mob.

As he comes closer, he shoves the hat away from his face. It's Pablo Montoya, the man who sat in her grandfather's parlor two nights ago. The man who was so angry with Americans and "that Bent." Alma shivers.

He stops at the edge of the crowd, hands on his hips. "¡Tontos!" he yells. "Fools! What are you doing here?" He glares at one man in particular, a old thin man with no teeth. "You were to deal with Beaubien!"

Bile rises in Alma's throat. Beaubien. The only Beaubien male in town right now is Narciso. And Andrew is with him.

The old man says something in a low voice. Montoya shakes his head in disgust and waves his hand dismissively at the crowd. "Go home," he says. They stare at him, unmoving. "Go home!" he shouts.

Then they shift and he sees the bodies on the ground. "Peabody and Locke?" he yells. He moves closer, bends to look, then straightens. "Both dead." He takes off his hat and swings it as if shooing a cow, waving the mob away. "What kind of animals are you? You destroy our cause before it has even begun!"

"Grandfather?" Alma whispers. There had been a slight sliver of hope in her heart. Now it's gone. Yet, even as her legs threaten to give way, she reaches for the bar of the gate, to go to him.

Anamaria blocks her hand, her face unexpectedly tender, and the girl allows herself to be led numbly away as shadows fill the Peabody courtyard.

TERESINA

CHAPTER 21 – AFTERNOON, JANUARY 19, 1847
Taos, New Mexico

I don't remember much else. Rumalda, crouched beside an old bedstead in the far corner of the room, a black rebozo draped over her head and shoulders. She's almost invisible in the shadows. The crowd tearing at Father's clothes and slashing at his face and hands with their knives. The terrifying moment when they turned to consider us.

"Americano spawn!" a woman snapped, glaring at me. Josefa clutched me closer.

"They are mere children," my mother sobbed.

"You!" A man shoved forward, shaking his finger in her face. "You consorted with him." He pointed to my dead father in the middle of the room, then went to him and poked at the body with his toe. "The mighty one who knew more than the priest. Who wielded his authority with his own justice, that belonged only to himself. Pah!" He bent down and spit into the bloody face. "That for his justicia!"

He turned back to us, his eyes narrowing. "Your daughter is la esposa of that americano Boggs," he said to my mother. He swung his head. "Where is she? There in the corner, pretending to be one of us." He crossed the room, yanked the rebozo away from her clutching fingers, and tossed it to a nearby old woman, who stroked it with gnarled hands. "This one has better use for it," he said.

Then he stalked back to us and loomed over me and Josefa. "And you," he said to her. "Married to that Carson, the one who scouts for americano troops. Pah!" He spit into her face and she jerked back, squeezing me tighter in her arms. He scowled at me, then reached for my auburn hair. "Little bright-haired one," he cooed. He glanced at my mother.

"She looks americano, that one," someone behind him said.

"She's only a child!" Josefa snapped.

But then their attention swung to my brother. "And this one is already carrying arms," the man said. "I saw him with the shotgun."

Alfredo glared at him. "I'll—"

But Mother grabbed his arm. "¡Silencio!"

The old woman with the rebozo cackled with glee, then Rumalda launched herself from the corner and crossed to my mother. "I have no americano blood," she told the crowd. "Take me for los niños."

Josefa set me gently aside. "Go to your mother, pequeña," she whispered in my ear, and then went to stand beside Rumalda. "And me, also," she told the mob. She glanced at Rumalda's pale face and took her hand. "Since we are guilty of loving our husbands."

"There will be no more taking of lives!" A man with a weathered face, sharp eyes, and thin lips stood in the now open doorway to the Lashone courtyard. He was short and thin but he carried himself with authority. He was wearing a broad

brimmed leather hat which he didn't remove. He looked around the room, then said, "They have killed the Beaubien boy and the Jaramillo heir."

My mother made a choking sound.

"Pablo?" Josefa gasped.

The man turned to the old woman. "Take what you must of their belongings," he said. "But we do not kill women and children." He waved a hand at the crowd. "Go!"

As they began to disperse, he crossed to my father's body, made a snorting sound, then turned to my mother. "You will remain here," he ordered. He swung to look at the remnants of the mob as they straggled out. "No one will touch you!" He raised his voice as he said it. A man waiting to go through the wall turned and gave him a mocking salute, but the rest of the crowd only nodded without looking up.

The man nudged at my father's chest with his toe, then looked at my mother. "You will watch beside your husband," he said. "And consider his outcome and that of your brother."

"It is true then?" my mother asked. "¿Pablo está muerto?"

"Sí. That Pablo Jaramillo who must spend all his time with the likes of Narciso Beaubien and—" He broke off and glanced at my father's corpse. "Others greedy for our land." He turned back to her, his face stern as he looked meaningfully toward Alfredo. "You will use this time to consider how best to speak to your children of what has occurred."

Mother reached around Estefina to pull me into her arms as well. "Gracias, señor," she murmured.

The man nodded abruptly and stomped out, shutting the door behind him. Rumalda and Josefa went to the bedstead in the corner, pulled the mattress off, and began unwinding the ropes underneath and disassembling the frame.

"Alfredo," Rumalda said. He looked at her dully. She nodded toward the hole in the wall, then the hand-adzed wood of the bedposts and he crossed the room to carefully drag them around Father's body and into position to block the break. Dirt sifted down from the torn-up roof, but there was nothing we could do about that.

Suddenly, Estefina broke away from my mother and me, stumbled a few feet away, and vomited onto the floor. "Oh, pequeña," Mama said.

But she didn't go to her aid. Instead, she stared at my father's bloody corpse. "And Guadalupe, too." Then she put her hands to her face and wept as the iron smell of blood and acrid taste of vomit filled the little room.

ALMA

CHAPTER 22 – JANUARY 21, 1847
Taos, New Mexico

Two days later, Andrew has still not reappeared. The bodies of Jeremiah Peabody and Gerald Locke have been removed, but Alma doesn't know where. She and Anamaria are afraid to leave the house for fear of being set upon by the mob, remnants of which still pass up and down the street periodically, weapons in their hands.

Juan Pacheco has visited twice. The first time, he reported that Padre Martínez's house was surrounded by insurrectos demanding that he release the American he was protecting. The second time, Juan told them there was a battle going on at Simeon Turley's grain mill and distillery north of town. Anamaria listened to him with a grim face and dug deeper into the supplies in the root cellar.

Now Alma sits numbly in her grandfather's parlor and stares out the window, focusing on the sky, not the street. Someone tried to get in this way. There's a crack in one of the glass panes, where a thick stick or a rifle butt hit it. Another one is speckled with small chips, as if it's been caught by the edge of a shotgun blast. She stares past them, willing Andrew to come home.

Not that she's really home. She has a sudden overwhelming desire for the valley and Ramón. Then she shivers. The old man may be the only family she has left. Where is her brother? She covers her face with her hands. What will she do if he's gone, as well?

Then she hears a voice in her head. Her mother, clear as day. "Don't just sit there. Go find him."

Alma feels a chuckle forming in her throat. Yes, her mother wouldn't be sitting here moaning. She would be out searching. Alma takes a deep, steadying breath, pushes herself to her feet, and heads to the kitchen. When she tells Anamaria where she's going, the housekeeper stares at her, then nods.

"Juan was here," she says. "The bodies have been taken to the plaza. El padre has been asked to bury them." She smiles humorlessly. "He agreed in exchange for safe passage for the people he's been harboring. And for himself, I imagine." She glances toward the open window. "Wrap up well, it's cold out there."

Alma nods absently. Cold or warm, the weather means nothing to her. However, there is the possibility of trouble. She swathes herself in a long dark rebozo instead of her mother's green-and-yellow shawl. She arranges the fabric carefully, forming a deep hood over her head before she steps into the street.

There's no one there. The road to the plaza is empty. She takes a steadying breath, then moves toward it.

Alma stays on the edge of the frozen ruts churned up by the mob, avoiding the spot where her father and grandfather went down. Two nearby houses show signs of being attacked. The window shutters hang loose on one and there are axe marks on the outer gate of the other. She shudders and moves on.

And then she reaches the entrance to the plaza and stops, staring.

The bodies of eleven men lie in a neat row. Someone has closed their eyelids and crossed their arms over their chests. They look like Catholic communicants. She steps forward. Closer, steeling herself.

Across the square, an old woman in a black rebozo stands talking to Padre Martínez. She looks toward Alma and makes an impatient gesture. Alma moves closer to the men on the ground.

There, the third in the row, is her father. He lies next to her grandfather. The top of his head is bloody, as if someone tried to scalp him, then gave up. Alma stares at the clots in his black curls, then turns away.

Jeremiah Peabody's feet are bare. Someone has stolen his boots and socks. For some reason, the indignity of his naked toes brings tears to her eyes. "Oh, Grandfather," she whispers. She swipes a hand at her cheeks.

The right arm of the man next in line ends in a mangled black stump. It's January, but a fly lifts from the wound.

The man next to him has been scalped. A single long, light-brown curl remains behind one ear. He's been stabbed numerous times, and there's a gunshot wound in his chest. She doesn't recognize him, poor man.

She closes her eyes for a moment, then goes on. There's an empty spot just beyond the silent form of Pablo Jaramillo. She closes her eyes. Josefa's brother. And Ignacia's. They've lost so much. And so quickly.

She steadies herself. Narciso Beaubien isn't here. Is the empty spot his? Has his family retrieved him already? Luz was so proud of his college education, happy that he was coming home. How will she bear it? Then hope blooms in Alma's chest. Perhaps it's just an empty spot, what Juan reported is mere rumor, and Narciso is alive. And her brother, too.

Her fingernails bite into her palm and she takes a ragged breath and looks down the little row of corpses once again, her eyes flicking over the bodies of her father and grandfather. Andrew isn't here. She walks up and then back down the line, checking. There's no sign of him.

But her father. Her grandfather. She returns to them hurriedly, as if straying too far from their sides is a kind of betrayal. She forces herself to look into their faces. Her father's expression is calm enough, slightly surprised, but nothing else. Her grandfather's mouth is twisted in contemptuous fury. He who was so mild in life, so slow to pass judgement, died angrily.

Grief washes over her and Alma presses her fingers into her palms, the nails cutting through the mental haze, and forces herself to consider the possibility of the living. If Andrew isn't here, where is he?

She looks around the square. The old lady and the priest have disappeared. Alma takes a ragged breath and moves blindly toward the other side of the plaza and the church beyond. Surely someone there will know something.

When she enters the building, Padre Martínez is in a nearby corner, speaking quietly to two rebozo-covered women. When he sees her, he leaves them and comes toward her. His face, lit by flickering candlelight, is streaked with exhaustion. "Señorita," he says. "I am so sorry about what has occurred."

"Gracias," she murmurs. It isn't the time for recriminations, to remind him of his own words, the ones that riled the hearts of the rebels, los insurrectos.

"We will say a Mass for the dead tomorrow," he says. "The unbaptized ones are to be buried in the land donated by my housekeeper, the plot where your mother is interred."

She pulls back. To bury her father anywhere but his mountain valley seems like sacrilege. Then her shoulders collapse. What does it matter? Besides, her mother is already there.

He has misunderstood her gesture. "They are— were Protestant," he says apologetically. "Canon law forbids them from being buried in sacred ground." He peers into her unresponsive face. "We will pray for them at the Mass."

She looks away. This man gave the mob the rationale for acting as they did and then protected some of the prospective victims. She should be questioning him about what he's done. Remonstrating. Her mother would have been a barrel of words against his apparent hypocrisy. But she is too numb and weary for indignation.

And she needs his help. She looks into his face. "I don't know where my brother is. He went Monday night to warn Narciso Beaubien about the attack at the jail."

She has to stop then. Her lips don't want to form the words. Please God, let it not be true. She takes a breath. "They tell me Narciso is dead."

The priest nods. "The Beaubiens sent for his body early today."

"And my brother?"

He shakes his head, spreads his hands, palms up. "Forgive me, señorita. That I cannot tell you. I have seen nothing of him, nor heard anything."

She nods and turns away.

One of the women in the corner tries to speak, coughs, and then moves toward her, jerking the words out. "Your brother. He is Andrew, the grandson of Don Jeremiah?"

A spark of hope lights Alma's heart. "Yes, he is Andrew."

The woman's voice is ragged from weeping. "I believe I may have seen him this morning with one of the Beaubien girls in the courtyard of their casa."

Alma moves toward her gratefully, but the woman shrinks back and puts out a hand, holding her off. "Mi esposo, he was of the mob," she half whispers. "They say los soldados americanos are coming. He has gone south with the others to fight them." Padre Martínez puts a hand on the woman's arm as Alma nods to them both and turns to the door.

This too is grief. The fear of a woman who knows her husband has participated in something unspeakable but still feels herself a part of him. Knows the pain from which he acts, foresees the grief that will result from what he is doing. The horror she will live with the rest of her days. As will he, if he survives.

Alma stands for a long moment outside the church, then gathers herself and heads back to the plaza. She crosses without looking at the men lying in its center. The Beaubien casa faces the eastern side of the square. It's a big house, the high adobe walls thick and topped with prickly pear plants as a deterrent to thieves. Half the gate is missing, its thick boards splintered in two.

Luz meets her in the salon. Her head tilts to one side and her shoulders curve toward her chest. "My brother—" she says.

Alma nods. "I have heard the news. I—" Her questions about her own brother die on her lips. "It is too horrible."

Luz drops onto the chair beside her. "And we have heard nothing from my father. Mama has taken to her bed." She reaches for Alma's hands. "I was so grieved to hear what happened to your Papa and Grandfather."

Alma closes her eyes. "I saw it."

"Oh, mi amiga!"

A servant appears in the doorway. "Señora Lee has arrived," she says gravely.

Luz rises, crosses to the door, and returns a few moments later with Benigna, whose blond hair has lost its curl. She's pulled it back into a careless bun at the nape of her neck. Alma looks into her eyes, then the two fatherless girls turn away from each other, both reminded of their own loss by the other's grieving face.

"We have not yet heard from Papa," Luz tells them. She covers her face with her hands. "I cannot bear it." Then she lifts her head. "At least we know where Narciso is and what has happened to him, horrible as that is."

"Yes." Alma turns to her. "My brother was on his way to him that morning, to warn him—"

"Oh, he arrived here. In fact, he brought the news of what occurred at the jail." Luz makes an impatient gesture. "They were on their way out to consult with Pablo Jaramillo when he came to tell us what had happened at the Bent house." She shudders. "Then we heard shouting in the plaza, Narciso bolted the gate and yelled at me to go inside, and the three of them disappeared into the stables."

There's a long pause. "And then?" Benigna asks. "Was it like what happened to my father? Did los insurrectos pursue them?"

"I went inside and bolted the door, but I could hear them at the gate, battering it down. Then they rushed in and began howling. Someone called to them from the roof. A woman, I think, and they headed off toward the stables. I hoped perhaps Narciso and the others had time to flee—" She rubs her hand over her face, then looks at Alma. "They dragged him and Pablo out into the muddy snow when they were done. I don't know what happened to Andrew."

Alma nods, her mind numb with Luz's story. Benigna touches her hand. "Perhaps he is at the priest's house. In one of the other rooms."

Alma gives her a confused look. "El padre, he harbored us," Luz explains.

Benigna nods. "We went out that afternoon to try to learn what was happening. We were crossing the plaza when los insurrectos surrounded us."

Luz closes her eyes. "Some of them were our neighbors." Her face twists as she looks at Alma. "I don't understand it."

"But Padre Martínez came and ordered them away," Benigna continues. "Then he took us to his house, where he hid us and some others. Only this morning did he determine it was safe for us to return home." She turns to Luz. "Ignacia and the children are still in the Lashone casa. An old woman stopped me from getting closer. She said not to draw attention, but that they are alive." She turns to Alma. "She also said messengers have been sent south and the americano soldiers are coming."

Alma nods numbly as Luz says bitterly, "Who knows if it is true." She closes her eyes. "How I wish my father was here. To know that he is safe is all I desire."

Alma nods in acknowledgement, but her stomach twists so that she can hardly keep herself upright. "I was told Andrew might have been here this morning," she says.

Luz frowns in confusion and shakes her head.

Alma's shoulders drop in defeat. "No one here has seen him?"

"The person who told you must have been mistaken," Luz says gently.

Alma nods. Weariness overwhelms her and she can barely make herself heard when she says her goodbyes.

TERESINA

CHAPTER 23 – JANUARY 23, 1847
Taos, New Mexico

I recall little of the hours that immediately followed my father's death. It still seems a horrible dream. But a dream with smells. My sister's vomit. Father's blood. The sharp stink of urine as first Alfredo, then I, were forced to relieve ourselves in a large pot Rumalda found in the corner. Josefa stood between us and the others, giving us a sense of privacy, her brown eyes huge in her pale, tear-stained face.

Light filtered in through the gap in the roof, so we knew when one day ended and the next began. We huddled together on the mattress on the floor, trying to keep warm. Twice there were taps on the door to the Lashone courtyard.

The first time, silent men removed my father's body for burial.

"Guadalupe?" my mother murmured and the oldest one nodded at her. "We have taken her," he said.

Mother flinched. "¿Muerta?"

He nodded and they went out. Mother turned to Rumalda. "Guadalupe," she said, tears in her voice. "That good woman." Rumalda pulled her into her arms.

Much later, there was a scratch, then a light tapping, on the boards. We all froze, then Josefa scrambled up and cautiously opened it halfway. Unknown hands thrust a bundle of clothes and another of food into her hands.

These gifts were accompanied by hurried news of others who had died at the rebels' hands. The sheriff. James Leal, the curly haired blond man with the supercilious look. And my godfather, Cornelio Vigil.

I still can't quite believe they killed him. The prefect, of all people. The news sent me to my mother's skirts, my thumb firmly in my mouth to stifle my cries.

Then we waited, not knowing what was occurring beyond the walls of the Lashone casa. Walls that seemed very fragile, for all their thick adobe construction. The hole in the roof let in the cold and occasional clumps of melting snow. We clung to each other, Josefa and Rumalda barely speaking, my mother whispering fragments of the rosary, my sister reeking of vomit, and my brother muttering, "I should have shot them," in hopeless, dull fury.

On the third day, an old friend of my mother's arrived. She was bent with age, but her eyes were sharp and her nose wrinkled in disgust at our smells.

"Doña Catarina!" my mother said, rising for the first time from her spot on the bed. "You shouldn't be here! They will attack you!"

"Let them try," the old lady said. She waved a gnarled hand. "Come. This is no place for you or los niños."

"But—"

"Rápido. Sin discusiones." She turned to Rumalda and my aunt. "Not you. Señor Manuel Gregorio Martin will come to

escort you to his casa." Her eyes crinkled with amusement. "He says you can help in the kitchen."

The two girls looked at each other. Josefa took Rumalda's hand and nodded to Doña Catarina. "Whatever you think best."

"I won't leave them here alone," Mother said.

"There is no need, señora." An old man appeared in the still half-open door. Mother and Doña Catarina jerked toward him. "Maldición! You startled us!" the señora said.

He sniffed at her, came inside, and pointedly shut the door. It was the man who'd led those who took Father's body away. He was tall and sparsely built, and had thin, sorrowful lips and eyes that squinted as if they had seen too much sun.

"Buenas noches," he said politely to my mother, but didn't wait for her reply. He turned to Tía Josefa. "You must come with me, señora. You and your niece." He turned to Rumalda and spread his hands. "I apologize for the abruptness of my speech, but there is no time for politeness." He looked around the room. "Do you have coverings?"

Rumalda went to the mattress, which held the rebozo that had protected her three days before. "There is this."

"Bueno." He turned to Josefa. "And you, señora? It is not safe for you to be in the streets without a covering."

Estefina, who was curled up on the bed under a small blanket, made a strangled sound, then sat up and held it out. "Take mine," she said.

The adults all turned to her. She gazed back at them with big eyes, holding out the blanket as she reached for our mother with the other hand. "Take it," she whispered. "Quickly."

"Yes, quickly," Doña Caterina said. She grabbed the blanket, thrust it at Josefa, and waved them toward the door. She

pointed up at the hole in the ceiling, where clouds obscured the light from the moon. "We must all be gone while it is well dark."

Señor Martin moved to the door, opened it, and peered out. Josefa and Rumalda started toward him, then turned back to embrace Mother and us children. "Be careful," Rumalda whispered as she bent over me, but Josefa didn't speak, only squeezed me tightly, as if leaving me was the most difficult thing she'd ever done. I caught my breath, doing my best not to cry, and she patted my cheek, then was gone.

Mother hurriedly collected the few clothes we had and wrapped us up as well as she could, but then the señora made us wait another long minute while she inched the door open and crept across the courtyard to peer into the street. Finally she beckoned us into the night air.

It felt so clean. The clouds had shifted and there was more light now. Doña Catarina frowned at the moon, but I was grateful. The shadows between the buildings were black and full of menace, but at least the immediate path before us was clear enough. The señora led the way, while Mother shepherded us from behind.

Somewhere a dog barked, and I startled and grabbed Estefina. "I think I'm going to be sick," she muttered, but the señora hissed "¡Silencio!" at her and we went on through the dark streets.

ALMA

CHAPTER 24 – JANUARY 27, 1847
Taos New Mexico

And then Alma waits. Her stomach is a solid stone, her muscles stiff with fear. There is nothing to do but try to move through the endless hours and strive not to think about what has happened, what may still be occurring. The absence of her brother weighs more on her spirits than that of her father and grandfather, as painful as that is.

Alma finds herself talking to her mother instead, holding whole conversations with her, returning again and again to that scene in the street. She should have done something, run out with a pitchfork and protected her men. But then, in her head, her mother snaps, "Don't be a fool! Did you want to die with them?" and Alma covers her face with her hands, although she still does not weep.

In the kitchen, Anamaria moves steadily through her tasks, but her heart is clearly not in them. The tortillas are either undercooked or burnt, and there's no salt in the stew. The gate to the street is well barred, but she jerks to attention at the slightest noise beyond it. Her hair remains down in a long braid, as if it carries its own set of grief and fear.

The two women do not speak. There's nothing left to say. When Juan appears, slipping between the corrals behind the house and then through the chicken shed, he knocks tentatively, as if unsure of his welcome.

He has nothing to tell them but rumors. The Americans are coming or have left the country entirely. Los insurrectos are going out to meet them, the men of New Mexico flocking to their cause. All of Taos Pueblo is in hiding. Charles Bent's wife and children have been captured and slaughtered in the fields. They are safe in Padre Martínez's house. Martínez is shielding others, as well: the brother of Luis Lee, Ignacia Jaramillo's son.

Finally, Anamaria tells him to stop bringing news of events he hasn't seen with his own eyes. He looks at her, clicks his tongue, and falls silent. But he continues to return at odd moments. To bring a brace of rabbits. To ensure the gate is truly blocked. To tend to the mules. He speaks now of only the simplest topics: the weather, the snow on the mountains, the condition of the animals in the corral, food for the poultry.

A strange, waiting hush settles on the casa, as it has on the town. The entire valley of Taos holds its breath.

And then one morning, the silence in the Peabody house is shattered by a pounding at the gate. Anamaria hurries out to open the little hatch, the shotgun tucked under her arm, Alma behind her. The housekeeper slaps the little shutter aside, peers out angrily, then pulls back, looking confused.

Ramón's anxious face appears in the aperture. Alma feels the clouds lift. "It's Ramón!" she says. She fumbles at the crossbar, then lifts it away and swings the gate open as Anamaria moves back, still holding the gun.

Chaser IV follows the old man into the courtyard. Alma falls to her knees and wraps her arms around his neck as he sniffs at her, then licks her face. "Chaser!" Tears well into her eyes.

And then, behind them, there's a shadow in the street. Andrew appears. Anamaria gasps, then shrieks, "Young man! Where have you been?"

But he doesn't have a chance to answer, because Alma has dashed to him and is wrapping him in her arms, regardless of how he might feel about being hugged in sight of anyone passing by.

Andrew nods to Ramón, then pulls away from Alma's embrace and gives her a troubled look. "I wasn't sure it was safe to come out until I saw Ramón." He bends to pet the dog.

The old man adjusts the snowshoes and pack slung over his back and turns to Alma. "He has not been here?"

Alma shakes her head and moves into her godfather's arms as Anamaria closes the gate. The housekeeper flaps her hands at the others, shooing them inside. "It is cold," she says. She glances uneasily toward the street. "And who knows who is listening?"

They go into the house, where Ramón drops his things just inside the door and they settle themselves in the kitchen. He reaches across the table to cover Alma's hands with his own.

"I started out as soon as I heard of the uprising," he says. He looks around the room. "Where is your father and Señor Peabody?"

The two women look at each other. Andrew, beside Alma, takes a deep breath.

Ramón pulls back, staring at them. "¿Él está muerto?" His mouth works soundlessly and he swallows. "Both of them?"

Alma nods. It's all she can do.

Andrew gestures toward the street. "Out there," he says. "I saw— I saw their bodies." He looks away. "That's when I ran."

Alma turns to him.

He glances at her, then away. "I was afraid." He looks at Anamaria. "Afraid of what I would find here. I hid, but I watched the house and I saw Juan coming and going, and the smoke from the kitchen fire. I didn't know—" He covers his face with his hands.

Alma turns to Ramón. "Andrew wasn't home that morning," she explains. "We had news of the sheriff's death the night before and he went to warn Narciso Beaubien."

"The man who brought the news told only of the death of Bent and Lee and Cornelio Vigil," Ramón says. He looks at Andrew, who lifts his head. "Narciso, also?" he asks. "You were too late?"

"I was there."

They all stare at him, waiting, but he shakes his head and turns away.

Ramón looks at Alma. "And you? When your father—"

"We were at the gate," Anamaria says. "She wanted to go to them, but I prevented her."

A tiny smile touches Ramón's eyes. "Sí, she would do such a thing. Thank you for stopping her."

Alma's chin lifts. "Surely—"

"No," he says gravely. "A mob is a wild beast. It cannot listen to reason or be restrained. The señora did right." He studies the two young people. "And I think it is too soon yet for me to hear from your lips what occurred."

Alma nods as Andrew shifts beside her, then stills. Ramón turns to the housekeeper. "Do you have what you need? Food? Firewood? The animals are safe?"

She nods. "My son has seen to us."

Andrew grimaces and Ramón gives him a sharp look. "Yes?"

"He is a rebel," Andrew says. "I saw him in the street with the others."

"You saw him strike Gerald and Señor Peabody?"

"No. He hung back toward the plaza. But he was there."

"That is little evidence on which to accuse a man. No one knows the heart."

Alma twists slightly, remembering the Paiz men that day, Manuel moving forward, Ysidro pulling him back. Then she shudders and covers her face with her hands. It's all simply too much.

Ramón pushes back from his seat. "Come," he says. "Let us rest and then we will tell the remainder of our stories."

Alma looks at him, suddenly guilt stricken. "You must be tired from your journey, and hungry as well. And I have thought only of my own grief."

His face twists. "The news you have given me is more painful than an empty belly." He swings away from the table and gestures toward the door. "I— I would like to reflect on it before we speak further."

She nods, her eyes suddenly filling with tears. He looks so weary, standing there. So old.

"I'll carry your things for you," Andrew says, rising from the table. Alma stares at her hands. Chaser pads in from the hallway and nudges at her lap. Anamaria looks at the dog suspiciously and Alma strokes his head, then rises to follow the others from the room.

* * * *

"I saw them kill Narciso and Pablo," her brother says abruptly. They're in the parlor, Andrew and Ramón facing the fire, Chaser drowsing in the corner next to Alma, who's holding one of her grandfather's law books. She looks up at her brother, but he's leaning forward to add another log to the fire.

"Narciso wanted to show us his new horse. Pablo Jaramillo arrived about the same time I did, and we both told Narciso that a mob was gathering, but he didn't seem to understand what was happening. He kept talking about his horse." Andrew shakes his head. "I suppose he'd forgotten a great deal while he was at that college in Missouri. He was remembering only the good things about Taos, about Nuevo México."

"Much has changed since he went away," Alma says. "Even while he was on his way back." She runs a finger over the book's embossed spine. "Since the American troops arrived last Fall."

Andrew nods. "Even up there in the valley, we felt it. Remember the way Padre Martínez spoke of los americanos? The triumphant attitude of Charles Bent when he came through last spring?"

Alma shoots him a quick look. She hadn't realized her brother had been paying that much attention during those visits.

Ramón tilts his head at Andrew. "You were with him and Pablo when it happened?" he asks.

Alma looks up, then back down at the book. She's been afraid to ask this question. The details of what Andrew experienced in the Beaubien shed have seemed untouchable. She wants to know, yet she's not sure she's ready to hear his story.

She closes her eyes. In the street outside, someone shouts a greeting and she jerks involuntarily.

She takes a deep breath. The men don't seem to have noticed the sound. Andrew leans forward to pick up the fireplace poker and maneuver an outlying log closer to the center of the flames. When he sits back, he glances at Ramón, then away. "We were in the courtyard when the mob formed outside the gate. Narciso ignored them and kept talking about his horse. But Pablo and I both interrupted and told him we needed to get out of sight. Luz had poked her head out the door. Pablo yelled at her to get inside and we headed toward the stables."

He takes a breath and goes on. "The mob was getting louder. I heard the gate smash, and someone yell, 'Where are they?' A woman answered. It sounded like she was on the roof, which was odd. Then I heard her call 'stable,' and I knew we were in trouble. Pablo and I headed for the shed where they keep the extra wagon and the hay. I thought we'd be safer there. I guess he did, too."

Andrew's hands grip the arms of his chair, his eyes on the fire. "Narciso turned back, but Pablo grabbed at him, hauled him in after us, and slammed the door. I dove behind the wagon and started piling straw over myself. I was hissing at them to hide when the door boards shattered. Someone had picked up a small log and was using it as a battering ram." He stops, staring into the flames.

There's a long silence. Alma looks at him, as manly and beautiful as ever in the firelight. The broad shoulders, the creamy brown skin and blond curls. He's changed since the shed. His eyes are sadder now, his mouth guarded. Her sweet baby brother. She has a sudden urge to go to him, pull his forehead to her, and kiss it the way she did when he was a toddler.

But that brother is gone now. There's no returning to what once was. She knows this with a bleak certainty.

Andrew begins again, his voice flat. "I crouched down behind the wagon, but I could see well enough through the cracks in the side boards. Narciso hesitated in the center of the room, but Pablo was moving toward me when an old man with wild hair yanked the door open. Pablo turned around and went back to Narciso. The old man had a stick in his hand as thick as my wrist." He glances at Alma. "Manuel Paiz was right behind him."

Alma stares at him. "Manuel Antonio?" she whispers.

He nods grimly. "He was looking over the old man's shoulder." He pauses, looks away. "Narciso always liked Manuel. They were good friends before Narciso left for school. Narciso used to go visit him at La Joya."

His voice changes. "Or I thought they were friends. Narciso smiled the way he always did, so delighted to see someone he liked, and moved toward Manuel with his hand out."

Andrew turns to Ramón. "Then the old man hit Narciso on the head with the stick." His voice is filled with disbelief. "He lifted it and swung sideways and crashed the stick into the back of Narciso's skull." Andrew swallows, the firelight glinting on his throat. "Narciso didn't fall over. He just— collapsed."

He puts his head back and goes on talking, but more to the ceiling than the others. "Then they all came crowding into the shed, and I couldn't see what was happening, but there was a kind of gurgling sound and then blood spattered the walls. It—" He stares up at the latillas. "Some of it hit the ceiling. I thought I was going to be sick."

There's a long pause, the crackle of the fire loud in the room, then Andrew goes on. "It got real quiet. Then someone near the wagon growled 'Había tres' and I was sure I was next." Alma sucks in her breath and he flicks a reassuring smile at her. "All of a sudden, a man outside yelled, 'They got Bent!' and everyone took off." He lowers his head, takes a deep breath, and looks at Ramón. "When I came out from behind the wagon, I saw they were both dead. Their throats had been slit."

"Pobrecitos," Ramón murmurs.

There's a long pause. Andrew stares at the fire. "They were my friends and I didn't help them. I hid while they died."

Alma's fingertips grip the book in her lap as if they're afraid to let go. "You would have been killed too." She swallows the tears in her throat. "The mob was too big and too wild. You couldn't have saved either of them."

"I tell myself that. Every night." He raises a shoulder. "Every hour. It doesn't help."

There's a long silence. Alma opens her grandfather's book, smoothing the thin paper, but she doesn't look down at the words. Her eyes sting with unshed tears.

"Pablo was my friend," Andrew goes on. "Even though he was so much older than me. And Narciso. I was looking forward to hearing about what he'd learned at his college."

"You lost so much that day," Alma says, knowing how inadequate this is.

"We all did." A note of bitterness creeps into his voice. "Except Manuel Antonio Paiz."

Alma turns away. Her stomach twists again.

Ramón stirs and tilts his head to the side and studies the fire. "Manuel, as well," he says gravely.

Andrew grunts and stands up. "I'm going out to check on the animals." The big dog rises and goes with him.

TERESINA

CHAPTER 25 – JANUARY 29, 1847
Taos, New Mexico

We didn't celebrate the anniversary of Alfredo's birth that year. I'm not sure he even remembered that he was now ten. Doña Catarina was kind, but the days merged together in a long dark tunnel, punctuated by meals we barely touched. We children slept a great deal, though our dreams were troubled. I wonder now if the women put something in the tea they gave us, manzanilla perhaps. Or something stronger. They say sleep is a great curative.

Either my mother didn't take the medicine she gave us, or it wasn't sufficient to calm her. She sat a great deal, staring at the high, wood-barred windows, listening to the street noises, murmuring "Guadalupe" over and over again, and fretting about my half sister and aunt.

When Señor Martin appeared one day, she leapt to her feet. "My daughter?" she asked. "And Josefa? They are safe?"

He smiled at her, his lips bending almost as if in spite of themselves. "They are well. They have become quite adept at grinding corn with the mano and metate."

She tilted her head questioningly.

"When visitors come to the house, they must pretend to be servants," he explained. "It is safer that way. No one looks at an Indian in the corner grinding corn."

My mother nodded uncertainly.

"They practice each day," he continued. "DoñaJosefa insisted they do so. She worried that anyone who looked carefully might notice clumsiness on their part and suspect the truth."

My mother nodded distractedly. "And the town?" she asked. "Do rebels still roam the streets?" She looked up at the little open-air window. "I sometime hear noises—"

He shook his head. "Los insurrectos still roam the valley of Taos, but the town itself is quiet. Many have gone south to fight los soldados americanos."

Beside me, Alfredo jerked upright. "The American soldiers? They are coming?"

"So I am told." Señor Martin spread his hands, palms up. "Certainly, the rebel leaders seem to believe it. Pablo Montoya and Tomás Romero have taken men and arms to turn them back at La Cañada."

My mother shuddered. "More death."

His narrow face dropped into its usual sorrowful lines. "Sí, señora. Almost certainly, more death."

Estefina, who had been curled into a ball on the bed beside Alfredo, sat up. "Mama, my stomach—"

"Yes, my darling." As my mother crossed the room to us, Doña Catarina came in carrying a tray with fragrant cups of hot chocolate.

"Mama!" Estefina whimpered.

Mother, leaning toward her, looked over her shoulder at the other adults. "Forgive me," she said. "My children—"

They nodded and went out. Mother sat on the bed and put her arms around us. "The American soldiers are coming," she said reassuringly. "We will not always live in this room. They will come and make the rebels stop, and then we will see your sister and aunt once again."

Then she gave me a stern look. "Teresina, take your thumb out of your mouth. What will Josefa say when she sees that you have turned into a big baby?"

Estefina giggled and Alfredo snorted, but I simply looked at them, thumb between my lips, and sucked harder. Mother pulled me closer and kissed the top of my head. "My poor little ones," she murmured. "My angels."

ALMA

CHAPTER 26 – JANUARY 29, 1847
Taos, New Mexico

Alma is in the courtyard, drawing water from the well, when there's a knock at the gate. She set the bucket down, crosses the courtyard, and opens the little hatch. Rafael Luna smiles at her from the other side.

"Buenos días," he says cheerfully. He glances over his shoulder at the street behind him. "I hope you are well."

She stares at him. Time has stood still since she last received a social call. She doesn't remember the appropriate response.

His face changes, gentles. "I come with news which may be of interest to you," he says quietly.

She nods and moves to lift the bar from the gate. He follows her silently to the well, lifts the water bucket, and carries it into the house.

Anamaria greets him politely, shows him where to place the water, and shoos them both out of the kitchen. Alma leads the way to the parlor. When Rafael sinks into her grandfather's favorite chair, she stifles a protest, then sinks into the one opposite, where her father used to sit. Their absence is an unusually heavy weight this morning. She folds her hands in her lap and waits for her visitor to speak.

"You have lovely eyes," he says abruptly.

She looks up at him. "¿Qué?"

He flushes. "Please accept my most abject apologies, señorita. I—"

She shakes her head, smiling faintly. "I have forgotten the ways of society," she says. "It seems so long ago that we spoke in that friendly, bantering tone."

He nods somberly. The firelight glints on his dark curls. "Yes. Much has occurred in the last ten days."

They both stare at their hands. Finally, he speaks again. "I bring news I believe will be of interest to you. Ignacia and her children are safe, of course, protected by the strong ferocity of Catarina Lovato."

Alma smiles faintly. "Yes, Anamaria's son told us. I doubt anyone will attempt to cross Doña Catarina's threshold." Then she frowns. "But you said Ignacia and her children. What of Josefa?"

"She and Rumalda have been in another location. I believe they go to Catarina's home soon now."

She nods absently.

"And Benigna—"

Alma glances up. "Oh yes, Benigna. How is she?"

"Her husband has returned and she feels safe enough. I saw her at the market in the plaza this morning, buying dried squash to replenish her stores." He shakes his head, his eyes dark. "The rioters did more than kill people. They stole everything they could find."

Alma shudders, thinking of the invasion she and Anamaria had managed to avoid, and clutches at a less difficult subject. "There is food for sale in the plaza?"

"Sí, although not a great deal."

"I should go and see what they have. Anamaria and I haven't ventured out to shop since—" She swallows and goes on. "That day."

He gives her a sympathetic look. "If you do not feel you are ready, perhaps I can be of assistance."

She closes her eyes, then opens them. "I must make myself ready."

He nods, then leans forward. "May I escort you?"

She pauses, the fog lifting slightly from her heart. His offer is tempting, but he's leaning forward too eagerly. Appearing in the street with him would be an announcement to the entire valley that he's courting her. She's not ready for that.

She shakes her head. "This is something I must do myself," she says apologetically. Her spine straightens. "To prove to myself that I can."

He nods and leans back, accepting the explanation. "Perhaps I may visit some other day?" he asks hopefully. "To converse on more pleasant subjects?"

She smiles in spite of herself. "Perhaps."

Ramón comes in just then, followed by Andrew, and Rafael stands to greet them. "I was just leaving," he tells Ramón. Then he turns to Alma. "I did have one more bit of news."

She braces herself as he goes on. "The rebellion was not confined to Taos and the attack on Turley's mill," he says. "Americano traders were killed at Mora."

They all stare at him. He spreads his hands, his eyes suddenly weary. "My people are foolish. These were men returning with wagons to Missouri. No one seems to know why they were attacked. But they are all dead."

Alma closes her eyes as Ramón, who never swears, mutters "¡Maladicion!" and Andrew says, "So the Army will go there also?"

"I think so, yes."

"How long will we have to wait here?"

Alma opens her eyes. She's never heard him speak so restlessly.

Rafael shakes his head. "If they arrive," he says. "Los insurrectos went a few days ago to face them at La Cañada. I have heard nothing since then."

"And yet life must go on," Ramón says.

Alma nods, takes a deep breath, and rises from her seat. "And there is food being sold in the plaza, so that it may do so," she says. "I must consult with Anamaria about what is needed to replenish our stores."

"When you venture—" Ramón says.

"I'll go with—" Andrew says at the same moment.

But Alma smiles and shakes her head at them all. She lifts her chin. Her mother would have gone out on her own. She can, as well.

* * * *

Alma stands for a moment outside the Peabody gate. The air is different here, less closed in than the courtyard and smelling more of mud than firewood. Her eyes flick over the spot where her father and grandfather died, then she turns resolutely to the right, her shoulders stiff as she heads toward the town plaza.

There she finds several vendors from the pueblo. She buys strips of dried pumpkin, then heads inside the Beaubien store to purchase salt. Everyone she interacts with seems quieter than usual, more subdued. As if they, too, are waiting to see what happens next.

Or maybe it's because so many of the men have headed south with the rebel leaders. She frowns, remembering that Rafael Luna had said Tomás Romero was one of them. It's hard to believe. She wishes she had some way to confirm that the man who came to her grandfather for advice is now leading the people who killed him.

She shakes her head. It's all too much to take in. She steps into the plaza and turns right, toward the eastern exit. Then she hears a voice behind her. "¿Señorita?" it asks.

Her stomach reacts before her brain fully processes the voice. She turns slowly. Yes, it is Manuel Antonio Paiz. He stands looking at her anxiously as he brushes his straight dark hair away from his forehead.

"You are well?" he asks.

She nods, her mouth suddenly dry.

"And your brother? I heard that he went missing a good while."

"Yes," she says. "He was afraid of what you all might do to him."

He stares at her. "I?"

"You and your friends. Los insurrectos."

He shakes his head, but she continues. "I saw you, that day. In front of—" She turns her head, blinking away the sudden tears, forcing her grief to become anger. "In the street outside my grandfather's casa."

He goes still, his eyes wide, and wets his lips with his tongue. "I tried to stop them."

"It looked to me like you wanted to help."

"You saw?"

She nods, suddenly mute.

"Oh, señorita." There's real pain in his voice. "I am grieved for you. To see such a thing." He reaches toward her but she flinches away. "I wanted so much to stop what was happening, but it was beyond my control."

"And were the deaths in the Beaubien shed also beyond your control?" It's as if her mother speaks through her, that sharp precision of tone.

He flinches a little. "I did not participate in their killings, though I do not condemn the outcome of that event."

"You think they should have died? Been murdered?"

He spreads his hands, palms up. "Ah, is it murder to eliminate a threat to one's very way of life?"

"Narciso Beaubien? A threat?"

"He was heir to his father and a participant in the theft of our land. The judge has stolen vast swathes to the east and participated with Luis Lee in the appropriation of more to the north, in Narciso's name."

Her lips tighten. "And Pablo Jaramillo? How is his death justified?"

He shrugs. "Señor Jaramillo was known to agree with los americanos about all things. He had made himself obnoxious with his talk."

"So you believe a man should die because he speaks his mind. Is that why my father and grandfather were killed?"

"Ah, señorita. I have already told you I disagreed with what happened there and tried to prevent it." He pushes his hair from his forehead again and spreads his hands. "The people were already irritated with the way los americanos have insinuated themselves into all aspects of our lives here. Marrying our women. Running las tiendas." He nods toward the Beaubien store and goes on. "Creating liquor to tempt us, like Simeon Turley. And now that the americano army has invaded our land, we despair of any recourse besides violence." He shrugs. "When Gobernador Bent refused to follow the traditional ways, the despair became anger and the anger exploded into a natural physical manifestation against all los americanos."

"Pablo Jaramillo wasn't American. And Narciso Beaubien was half Mexican."

"He was half norteamericano. His blood can't be trusted."

Alma stares at him, a hard knot in her stomach. She and her brother are half American. Are they also not to be trusted?

He seems to read the question in her face. "You are more of the American enslaved race," he says. "In many ways, you have as much right to hate them as we have." Then he smiles. "If I had found your brother beforehand, I would have asked him to join us at La Cañada and Embudo, where we gave los americanos a good fight. He could have come with me to visit my parents at La Joya."

She narrows her eyes at him. Surely he's joking. But he goes on, a slight smile on his face. "I would like to take you to meet them when this is over and we have pushed the Americans back to where they belong."

She stares at him. In New Mexico, a man invites a woman to meet his parents in order to get their approval about a possible courtship and marriage. She closes her eyes, opens them again, and shakes her head, trying to process what he's just said.

His smile fades. "But perhaps it is not to be."

"Perhaps not." She looks down at the purchases in her arms, then up at the sky and around the plaza. The days are still short this time of year. The shadows are beginning to lengthen and there's an icy edge to the air.

Padre Martínez comes out of the door of the one-story adobe courthouse on the north side of the square, and stands watching them. "I must return to la casa," Alma says. "Good day."

Manuel bows formally. "Good day, señorita."

She moves firmly toward the plaza entrance, but glances back as she reaches it. He's still standing there, looking forlorn. Revulsion twists her chest into a knot. He stood and watched her father and grandfather be murdered and now has the audacity to invite her to meet his parents. She takes a deep breath and turns to look up at the mountains that loom at the end of the street to her grandfather's house. They are covered with snow, an icy barrier to her valley. Tears well in her eyes.

At this moment, all she wants to do is go home.

CHAPTER 27 – FEBRUARY 1-3, 1847
Taos, New Mexico

Alma's longing for the valley doesn't fade. But when she tells Ramón how she feels, he shakes his head sadly. "The snow, it was so deep on the pass that I was forced to wear snowshoes," he tells her. "Not even a mule could get through that."

"Certainly not the wagon," she admits. "And more snow has fallen on the mountains just in the last few days."

"Sí, it is so. And then there is the matter of the papers for the land." A smile flickers across his tired face. "We must not return until we accomplis the task Suzanna set for us."

Alma chuckles. "She might haunt us if we don't," she agrees. Then her shoulders drop. "I miss her so much. And the valley."

"I know, nita. But it is not possible. We must wait to speak to Carlos Beaubien about the land. I expect he will follow close behind los soldados americanos."

"If they ever arrive," Alma says. "If the rebels don't beat them back."

The old man shakes his head. "The old muskets and pikes of los insurrectos will be inadequate in the face of the weapons of los americanos. The rebels may slow them down, but they won't be stopped."

She shivers. "And then there will be more blood."

"It is to be expected." He glances around the room, as if assessing the house's capacity to withstand gunfire. "There is some thought that los insurrectos may seek to block the soldier's path as they march in from the mountains."

Her stomach clenches. "In Don Fernando itself?"

He shakes his head. "I do not know. It is all talk. Nothing is certain."

Some certainty arrives the following Tuesday. Alma is in the plaza buying supplies when she notices local men streaming past the eastern entrance, north toward the pueblo. Rafael Luna, who's been standing watching them, turns as she approaches.

"Here you see the great army of rebellion and protection," he says, waving toward the tattered men. "They have encountered the guns of the American army, and now hurry to the protection of the pueblo walls."

"The walls there won't protect them. They aren't high enough."

"I believe they intend to make a stand in the church. After all, it was built to protect against Comanche attacks." His lips curl. "It is sheer foolishness." He looks down at her. "May I escort you across this flowing sea of humanity and see you safely home?"

She nods, and he puts a hand up to stop the oncoming men while he guides her across. Several of them nod to Alma politely, but others mutter and give her and her escort dark looks.

"They are not feeling hopeful," Rafael observes, his lips quirking. Then he turns serious. "Their despair will turn ugly very soon. I would advise you and your family to stay indoors during the next several days."

Alma shivers. As they reach the Peabody gate, she turns to him. "I hope you plan to do likewise."

His eyes sparkle with amusement. "Ah, you do care what happens to me!" he exclaims. "I would endure much danger for the sake of hearing you express your concern so readily!"

She narrows her eyes at him and nods toward the end of the street, where the rebels are still moving north. "This is not a matter for amusement."

His face sobers. "Sí, señorita. It is not." He looks into her eyes. "However, the fact that you express concern for my safety does warm my heart." He reaches for the gate and swings it open just enough for her to enter. "May God go with you," he says as he shuts it behind her.

She stands for a long moment, staring at the thick, hand-cut boards, then moves the bar into place and heads toward the house. Rafael Luna is a flirt and not to be taken seriously. But even he seems worried about what will happen in the next few days. She shivers. How will it end?

Her question is answered the next afternoon, when cannons begin thundering beyond the hills northeast of town.

Alma is in the parlor with her brother and Ramón, trying to read. The sky outside is gray, and little light filters through the thick-paned glass windows. She sits by the fire, the pages of her book tilted toward the flames, Chaser at her feet.

The two men look up at the sound of the big guns. "It has begun," Ramón says. Andrew flinches, then catches himself and goes back to whittling the small horse he's been working on the last few days.

The booming goes on steadily for over two hours, then suddenly stops. They look at each other. "Is it over?" Alma asks.

Anamaria comes in. "My son has news," she says. She makes a gesture toward the kitchen. "He is warming himself with coffee and stew."

They all troop after her to find Juan Pacheco hunched over a bowl of hot meat, vegetables, and broth. It isn't really time for a midday meal, but Alma helps Anamaria dish up and they all join him at the table.

"I have been in the hills outside the pueblo, watching in the snow," Juan explains.

Ramón nods. "Was your endurance rewarded?"

"I learned that the walls of that big adobe church can withstand americano shells as well as Comanche lances and guns."

The others stare at him. He nods. "They have at least one cannon, but los americanos accomplished only the expenditure of powder and shot on this day." He clicks his tongue. "What will happen tomorrow is another question."

Alma shudders as her brother says, "They'll keep beating at those walls until they crumble."

Ramón and Juan nod at him. "Almost certainly," the younger man agrees. "I saw no indication that los soldados planned to go away any time soon."

And so it is. The guns begin again the next morning and continue hour after long hour. Alma's body grows used to the bombardment and stops jerking every time there's another blast on the other side of the hills northeast of town.

It's like grief, she decides. After a while, the shock wears off and it's simply there, a constant companion, yet another adjustment made to accommodate events.

When the firing finally ceases late that afternoon, the sudden silence feels louder than the cannons had. Alma stops short in the middle of the kitchen, a bucket of well water dripping onto the floor, her head up. "Is it over?"

Anamaria's hands, submerged in the big bowl on the counter, have stilled. She listens, head cocked, then breathes out a long sigh. "I pray it has ended," she says.

They stand waiting, but the guns don't start up again. Ramón and Andrew appear in the doorway. The old man already has his coat and hat on.

"Please don't go," Alma says. "We don't know what has happened."

He looks at her sympathetically, but says, "I have waited here long enough. I must discover what faces us."

"I'll go with you," Andrew says.

Alma opens her mouth to protest, then shuts it. His face is more animated than it's been in days, although his expression is more anxious than excited. "Be careful," she says.

"Go with God," Anamaria tells them.

They return two hours later, Juan Pacheco with them. Together, they describe the death of the soldiers who tried to break down the church door, the maneuvering of the cannon ever closer to the thick church walls as the rebel rifles spit death onto the attackers. The grapeshot that finally shattered the adobe, the final assault.

And the killing outside the walls as the defenders tried to flee and los americanos on horseback, led by Ceran Saint Vrain, cut them down.

By the time they finish telling the story, Alma has covered her face with her hands. "It is too terrible," she whispers.

"How many died?" Anamaria asks.

Ramón shakes his head. "Perhaps two hundred all told. Many americano soldiers also lost their lives."

She shakes her head. "So many. And what have they accomplished?"

"Los americanos have indeed accomplished a great deal," her son says bitterly. "There is no doubt now that they rule this land."

She looks at him sternly. "As I have said from the beginning: it is sufficient to feel anger. A time comes when we must bow to events, no matter what we think of them."

"Sí, madre," he says wryly.

"Have the people of the pueblo accepted their fate?" she asks.

"There is to be a delegation tomorrow," Ramón tells her. "The women of the pueblo are meeting now, to decide who will participate."

"And—" Alma wets her lips with the tip of her tongue. "The men? Tomás Romero, for example?"

He shrugs, but Juan says, "I believe he still lives. I heard the American colonel saying he wants to take him alive, so he can be made un ejemplo of."

Alma stares at him. "An example?"

Ramón grimaces. "I expect he'll be hung."

She closes her eyes. "When will it end?"

TERESINA

CHAPTER 28 – FEBRUARY 3-7, 1847
Taos, New Mexico

We finally left Doña Catarina's house the afternoon the American soldiers arrived. In fact, they found us. Colonel Price came to pay his respects and escort us home. He designated a nice young man to help us put the casa to rights, then apologized for leaving so soon. "My scouts tell me the rebels are holed up in the church at Taos Pueblo," he said disapprovingly. "I must go and roust them out."

"They see the church as a place of protection," a voice said from behind him.

"¡Tía!" I shrieked, darting toward the door.

"Sister!" Estefina cried as she ran past me.

Rumalda hugged Estefina as Josefa removed my clutching hands from her skirt and dropped a curtsy to the colonel. Then she drew me closer while my mother made introductions.

"Ah, the wives of the famous Kit Carson and the almost as famous Thomas Boggs," Colonel Price said. He was a tall man with an air of command, but his smile and voice were friendly enough. Josefa and Rumalda nodded in pleasure that he knew the names of their men.

"I apologize for interrupting as I did," Josefa said. "But it may be helpful to you to know that los insurrectos see the church as a place of defense as well as worship."

Rumalda nodded agreement. "It was built very strongly," she said. "To serve as a place of safety from the Comanches. There are slits in the walls to allow the defendants to fire on attackers."

The colonel stared at her. "Firing from a church?" Then his face cleared. "So it is not considered a place of sanctuary."

She shook her head. "Not in the way churches are considered sanctuary in your country, no." He gave her a quizzical look and she shrugged. "It is a difference my husband finds interesting and so we discussed it."

"Ah." He turned to my mother. "I must go and investigate this phenomenon myself and determine how best to breach the building's defenses." He bowed himself out and we all clustered together in the middle of the room. "Tía," I breathed into Josefa's skirt. "I am so glad to see you again."

"Now you can stop sucking your thumb," Estefina said, and I made a face at her.

Rumalda laughed. "It is so nice to hear you bickering as usual," she said. She looked around the room. Chairs were overturned. There was a great scar in the table, where someone had taken a knife to it. The clothes chest had been turned on its side, its lid wrenched half off. "We must set all this to rights and get a fire started so we can cook some food."

The young man Colonel Price had left with us came in, his arms full of wood.

Rumalda smiled at him. "Ah, here is a man who understands what is necessary."

Mother wiped tears from her eyes. "It is so good to see you again, my daughter." She reached for Josefa. "I have missed you both so much."

We went to work setting things to rights, and the casa had begun to feel a little like home again when we heard the first booms northeast of town. We all stopped to listen.

Josefa turned toward the young man the colonel had left for us with a questioning look. "That will be our cannon fire," he said. "Those balls should make short work of that old church."

Mother and Rumalda exchanged bemused looks as Josefa said, "I pray it is so, that the bloodshed ends quickly."

Then the booming started again. I scrambled into the comfort of the adobe bench near the fireplace, and Estefina followed me. Alfredo eyed us with ten-year-old male disgust, then came and sat on the floor with his back to the bit of wall between us and the flames.

We stayed there all through that day and the next. The booming went on and on.

And then it was over. Our friend the soldier went out for a little while and returned to say the rebels were fleeing into the foothills pursued by men on horseback. My mother nodded quietly at this, but Alfredo jumped up and did a little war dance in the middle of the room. "Whoop!" he yelled. "Yippee!"

Rumalda chuckled, but my mother turned away. "So much death," she murmured.

"So it will be safe now to venture into the streets?" Josefa asked the soldier.

The young man squinted at her.

"We have seen little daylight these last two weeks," she explained.

He shifted uneasily. "Things are still unsettled. I reckon it'd be better if you waited 'til morning."

"Yes, please wait, sister," Mother said. She looked at me. "Teresina, your thumb."

I dropped my hand. Josefa nodded to my mother and the soldier. "I will go tomorrow," she said. She went to the fire, where she moved the cast iron skillet into place to begin heating it for the tortillas and looked over her shoulder at me. "I will want company to give me courage."

I stared at her, my thumb moving toward my mouth, then dropped my hand as I nodded. "I will go with you."

It was late morning the next day before we ventured out. The first person we met was Señor Beaubien, who looked pale and tired. He greeted us with a distracted air. "They tell me Tomás Romero has turned himself in," he said. "I'm going to the jail now, to see him safely incarcerated."

Josefa's forehead furrowed. "Couldn't someone else take that responsibility?"

He made a small, helpless gesture. "I am the judge. My son died at their hands, but still I am the judge."

She nodded, her eyes wide with sympathy.

"Would you come with me? Both of you?" he asked. He smiled down at me. "Your presence would give me great comfort."

Josefa looked down at me with a troubled expression, but when I smiled confidently back at her, she nodded. "We will come."

So we were there outside the jail when Tomás Romero was escorted around the corner from the plaza by a cluster of soldiers. A crowd had formed in the street, blocking my view, but I saw when Romero and his guard stopped moving. We stepped to one side, toward our front gate which was across the street from the jail, so we could see better.

Señor Romero leaned forward slightly, speaking to someone. I stood on my tiptoes. He was talking to Señorita Locke, who stood in the middle of the street, her rebozo looped around her shoulders. Her curly black hair looked as if it hadn't been combed in days. Her face was streaked with tears.

"What of your father and grandfather?" Romero asked her.

She shook her head.

"Both of them?"

She nodded.

"Forgive me, señorita," he said. "It was not what I intended."

"And yet it happened." She glanced at the jail just ahead and the battered wooden bench beside its yawning door. The soldiers guarding him. The onlookers. Her gaze returned to Romero.

"Is this how we are to live now? Hating each other? In constant fear?" She shivered and turned to look at our house. Don Carlos made a small gesture of recognition, but she didn't see him.

She turned back to the Taos leader. "My father and his father came to Nuevo México to be free." She pushed her hair away from her forehead. "To be treated like other men. They should have stayed in Missouri. They would probably be in chains, but at least they would be alive." Her voice broke then. She bent her head and pulled the nearest edge of her rebozo up over her mouth.

"Pobrecito," Josefa murmured. She moved forward impulsively, but Don Carlos put a restraining hand on her arm.

"Ramón is there just behind her," he murmured, and we watched the old man step forward and take the señorita's arm.

As they turned away, Luz Beaubien appeared. She raised her nose at the prisoner, then took Alma's other hand, and walked with her and Don Ramón up the street.

Don Carlos chuckled. "It's good to see that daughter of mine getting her haughtiness back." Then he looked toward the jail and the people crowding around it. The man at the head of Romero's guard detail spoke sharply, ordering people back, then the prisoner and his escort began moving again.

Don Carlos patted my aunt's hand and released it from his arm. "I realize now that I must do this myself," he said. "You should not be exposed to that crowd." He smiled at me. "But I thank you for your company."

He gave us each a little half hug and moved across the wide street to the jail. Josefa glanced at our house, then took my hand. "Come," she said. "Let us go for a little walk. Shall we see if Benigna is at home?"

I was exhausted when we returned and none of us ventured out again until Rumalda's Uncle Rafael came on Friday with news that the rebel leader Pablo Montoya was to be hung that afternoon.

"Only Montoya?" my brother asked. "What about that Tomás Romero who used to come here? The one who scalped my father?"

My stomach twisted. I didn't want to remember what happened that day.

Rafael laughed. "That one has been dealt with by the Americans already," he said. "Didn't you hear?"

My mother eyed Estefina and me, then said, "Should las niñas know about this?"

He grinned. *"They'll probably sleep more easily at night as a result."*

Rumalda frowned at him. "What happened?"

"Los soldados americanos captured Romero."

"And took him to the jail," I said. I looked at Josefa. "We saw it."

He nodded and raised an eyebrow at Josefa. "You weren't there when it happened?"

"¿Que?" she asked. "What was it that happened?"

"One of the americano soldiers shot him at the jail a few minutes after he arrived and killed him."

She stared at Rafael, looked at me, then closed her eyes. "We went for a walk," she said faintly. "Before he actually went into the building."

"Gracias a Dios," my mother muttered.

"I want to see Montoya hang," Alfredo said, his jaw jutting out.

"No," Mama said flatly.

She looked at my sister and aunt. "If you wish to attend, I won't try to prevent you. You are married women. You can do as you like."

Alfredo opened his mouth to argue, but she stopped him with a look. "There has been enough death." She looked again at my sister and aunt, then scowled at Rafael. "You will stay with them every minute."

He held up a hand. "Sí, Doña Ignacia. I will stay with them. They will be safe with me."

She turned and swept out of the room. Rafael turned to my sister. "Will she ever recover from this?"

"I doubt it," Rumalda replied.

ALMA

CHAPTER 29 – EARLY MARCH 1847
Taos, New Mexico

By early March, Taos has returned to some semblance of normality. Tomás Romero is dead at the hand of an American soldier and Pablo Montoya at the end of a hangman's noose. American soldiers patrol the streets, keeping everyone indoors after nightfall.

But Alma can't sleep. After her father and grandfather's deaths, the heaviness of her grief had swept her into nothingness each night, and she'd been grateful for the long hours of not remembering. But now, as the days lengthen and the snow begins to melt, she wakens with the birds outside her window.

This morning, as she lies listening to them, she suddenly longs for her mother. This is the time of year when the snow in the valley begins to thaw. Suzanna would become restless and frustrated right about now. The ground was still rock hard and it was far too early to plant, so she would spend hours drawing up lists of what should be sowed in which field and when. Eventually, she would go restlessly to her loom, Ramón and Gerald would exchange looks of amused relief, and the house would settle again.

Alma closes her eyes. "Oh, Mama," she whispers. Then she takes a deep breath and pushes herself upright. Her mother would never have laid here and felt sorry for herself. She would have done something.

But what? Anamaria doesn't seem to need or want help in the kitchen, other than the occasional armload of firewood or bucket of well water.

There are a few early flowers blooming along the courtyard's south-facing wall. Alma nods. She'll pick some to take to her mother's grave. She closes her eyes, forces herself to breathe. Also for her father's grave. And her grandfather's.

She sits for a long moment, absorbing her losses once again. Will the pain ever stop stabbing her at the most unexpected moments? Then she rises and moves toward the door.

But when she looks into the kitchen to tell Anamaria her plans, she finds the housekeeper sitting at the table, her face in her hands. She looks up as Alma enters. Her cheeks are streaked with tears. "They have taken him," she croaks.

"Who?"

"My Juan. Los soldados americanos have taken him." Anamaria makes a small, helpless gesture. "They say he was at the church. That he is a rebel."

"But he was here, coming and going, all through that time."

Anamaria nods, shakes her head, nods again. "Sí, it is so."

"Surely they will realize he is innocent and release him."

The housekeeper looks at her skeptically.

"There must be someone who can testify for him." Alma chews on her lower lip. "I will ask Ramón."

But before she has a chance to do that, Rafael Luna arrives with a dozen willow stems that are just beginning to bud. "I thought you might like to place them in a container and watch them come alive," he says. He smiles at her gallantly. "The catkins will be as soft as your skin."

Alma smiles at the extravagance of his words and turns away to place the gift on the table. "My mother used to do that," she says.

"Oh! Forgive me. I do not wish to raise painful memories." He reaches for the stems. "I will take them away at once."

She puts her hand on his arm. "No, don't take them. They will remind me of her and her love of all things that grow."

His face softens as he covers her hand with his. "And you, what do you love?"

She's tempted to say 'my valley,' but something stops her. She shrugs, turns away, and places herself in a chair near the fire. When she gestures toward the other one, he goes to it, moves it closer to her, and sits down.

He leans forward, looking into her face. "Shall I tell you what I love?"

When she doesn't respond, he leans back and studies the flames. "I love a pure heart, and dark, curly hair, and a heart shaped design on one cheek."

She flashes a surprised look at him.

He raises a cautionary hand. "No señorita, let me finish if you please." He glances at the door. "Before someone comes in."

Alma makes a slight negating motion with her head, but he's looking at the fire again. "I love a feminine shape and a soft voice. And a girl who speaks truly." He glances sideways at her. "A girl who would honor the house of mi familia if she chose to reside there."

Alma opens her mouth, then closes it. She doesn't know what to say.

He turns to face her. "Do you think you could choose to live in the same household with me here in Don Fernando de Taos? To be my wife?"

She begins to shake her head, but he stops her with a touch on her hand. "It is not necessary to decide immediately. Perhaps I will return tomorrow, and you can tell me if the idea is to your liking?"

She nods wordlessly and he lifts her hand, gently kisses her fingers, and goes out.

Alma sits staring into the darkening room. She's just received a proposal of marriage. From Rafael Luna.

She's too stunned to know what to make of his suggestion. He has shown a definite interest in her, but she thought he was just practicing his flirtation skills. After all, he flirts with Rumalda, who is married, and his aunt. Is he serious?

When Ramón comes in, she's still sitting in the big chair, her hands gripping the armrests, absorbing the shock. When he asks her how she is, she responds mechanically and, with a guilty sense of relief, tells him about Juan Pacheco being taken into custody.

His face tightens. "And you know for a certainty that he is not of the rebels?"

She starts to shake her head, then pauses. "He is Anamaria's son," she says.

Ramón's lips twitch, but he doesn't answer.

She stares at him, willing him to help, to find a way to rescue this particular prisoner.

Finally, the old man lifts one hand in a small, helpless gesture. "I will make inquiries."

"Thank you." She gazes into the dancing flames. What of Rafael Luna?

Ramón leans slightly forward, looking into her face. "Is the plight of this man the reason you sit here staring into the fire?"

She rouses herself. "What?"

"You have feelings for him?"

"Oh! No, I'm just tired." She gets up and wanders toward the door. "I think I will go to my room."

There, Alma lays on the bed and stares up at the latillas. There's a cobweb in one corner. She should get a rag and attach it to a stick, dust the spider away. Yet she doesn't move. She gazes into the middle distance, trying to decide how she feels. Rafael Luna wants to marry her. Does she want to marry him?

The next morning, as the birds begin to sing, she opens her eyes knowing the answer. She doesn't want to marry Rafael and she doesn't want to stay in Don Fernando de Taos, where any-one can be taken for a rebel. She wants to go home.

She has a moment of anxiety about how to break it to him, then shakes herself and sits up. Rafael may believe he's serious, but she doubts his heart will be broken for long. And Alma simply doesn't feel for him the way her mother did for her fa-ther.

Also, she wants to go home. More than anything in the world, she wants to return to her valley.

When Rafael shows up that afternoon, she tells him as gently as she can.

"Are you quite certain, señorita?" he asks. "I offer you a home surrounded by those who will value you and strive to make our lives pleasant. People like my niece Rumalda, who is kindness itself."

Alma nods. "Forgive me, señor," she says gently. "But yes, I am quite sure."

He turns away, his head bowed, then wheels back to her, tears in his eyes. "I will never recover from this rejection," he says dramatically.

In spite of her desire not to upset him, Alma's lips twitch in amusement. She forces them to be still. "I will pray that your heart suffers no permanent damage," she says soberly.

He heaves a deep sigh, moves to the table, where she has placed the willow stems in a battered tin pitcher, and gently touches one of the half-open catkins. "As soft as your skin," he murmurs.

Then he turns back to her and bows formally. "I thank you for the softness of your reply, señorita. And now I must bid you good day." When she nods, he turns and goes out the door, shutting it behind him with a thud, as if emphasizing how upset he is.

Alma crosses to the chair by the fire, sinks into it, shakes her head, and laughs softly. Rafael Luna is so dramatic. "If I were a gambler, I'd bet good money that he'll have a new sweetheart within a few weeks and, if she is willing, be married within the year," she says aloud. She grins, a great gladness flooding through her. "And I won't be here to see it, because I will be home."

But when she tells Ramón that afternoon that she wants to head back to the valley, he frowns. "Would you leave Señora Pacheco alone as she waits to know her son's fate?" he asks gently.

Alma catches her breath. Numbly, she shakes her head.

"We cannot leave her here alone while her son faces possible death," he continues.

Her eyes widen. "Death?"

He nods. "Like the other prisoners, Ramón Pacheco is accused of murder. The americano penalty for murder is death."

"Poor Anamaria," Alma says. "You're right. We can't leave her until we know the outcome of his trial. When is it to be?"

"Early in April. Don Carlos has been back and forth between here and Santa Fe ever since the army has arrived, but I understand he is to preside in the courtroom."

She stares at him, open-mouthed. "He is to be judge at the trial of men accused of participating in the rebellion that killed his son?"

The old man spreads his hands. "So I am told."

"I cannot imagine. He must be bowed down with grief."

CHAPTER 30 – LATE MARCH 1847
Taos, New Mexico

However, when Ramón, Alma, and Andrew finally meet with Carlos Beaubien about the title to the valley land, they find him more irritable than bowed down. As if all his grief has mutated into anger and pride, with nothing left over.

As she and the others settle themselves into chairs in the Beaubien reception room, Alma studies him thoughtfully. She wonders if Ramón has chosen the best time to approach the newly stricken father with their request. But when will there be a good time? Don Carlos's grief may linger for years as he adjusts to the fact that he now has no son.

Ramón begins by offering condolences for the Beaubien family's loss. "It will be a great hardship for you," he says sympathetically.

Don Carlos shoots him a sharp look. "My daughter's husband, Lucien Maxwell, has returned from his adventures in California," he says. "I can lean on him, at least. He's suggested that we send more settlers out to the grant east of here. I presume that's why you've come, to discuss what you've been doing there."

Ramón makes a gesture toward Andrew and Alma. "We wished to extend our condolences."

"And ask about the grant." His eyes slide over the young people, then refocus. His face softens. "May I extend my own condolences on the demise of your father and grandfather." He gazes at Alma. "I understand you were there."

Her throat tightens. "I saw."

He turns to Andrew. "And you— You were in the shed?"

Andrew nods, his eyes on the floor.

"Did you—"

"I didn't see much." The boy's face twists. "I heard—"

Don Carlos lifts his hand, his own face suddenly stiff. "It's enough to know there was at least one friend with him."

Andrew raises his head. "I wish—"

"It would do no good to have you dead as well." He glances at Alma. "Then what would become of your sister?"

"She would have Ramón."

"And the land which her parents and I carved from the wilderness," Ramón says.

Alma, uncomfortable with the way she's being discussed as if she isn't there, inserts herself. "The land which they cultivated for eighteen years." She turns to Don Carlos. "You remember. You discussed it with my father when you met in January."

A smile flashes across his face. "He said it was twenty."

She glances at Ramón. "Señor Chavez and he discovered it twenty years ago." She smiles. "Papa said that as soon as he saw it, he knew he would return." She looks into Don Carlos's face. "Which he did, with Ramón as his partner." She pauses. Should she say it? She plunges forward. "Which he did long—"

"Before Guadalupe Miranda and I requested the grant from Manuel Armijo. Yes, I know." Beaubien turns to Ramón. "Miranda has fled south to Mexico. I doubt he'll return. The formalities of any transfer are now complicated by his absence."

The other man nods. "Sí, señor. I understand that. It will take time to acquire his approval. At this time, I would be satisfied with a clear title signed only by you. We can obtain his signature when it is more convenient."

Beaubien's eyes narrow. He looks at Andrew, then Alma, then Ramón. "These are Locke's only heirs?"

"I swear it."

"Their names should appear on the documents."

"I agree most wholeheartedly."

Alma straightens. "We are each entitled to one quarter." She nudges Andrew, but he's staring dully at the floor.

"It should be thirds," Beaubien says.

She looks at Andrew again, hoping for some kind of response. When he doesn't look up, she focuses on Don Carlos. "Señor Chavez and my father were full partners."

"It is of no matter," Ramón tells her.

"It matters to me. Mother—"

His lips twitch and even Don Carlos smiles a little. She forges on. "Mother would never forgive me if your portion was less than it ought to be."

Suddenly, Andrew looks up at Beaubien. "When we were here in January, Father told you he and Ramón had gone half shares in the place."

They all look at him in surprise. His eyes drop to the floor, the lids heavy with exhaustion. Alma frowns. Is he sleeping at all? She needs to get him home. She turns back to the men. "So, we are agreed. One half to Ramón, one quarter each for my brother and me. The papers to be drawn up soon and signed by you, Don Carlos, contingent on Señor Guadalupe Miranda's concurrence."

Beaubien looks at Ramón, who grins and spreads his hands, palms up. "She is the daughter of Suzanna, is she not?"

"And there is to be no fee of any kind," Alma adds. "It would not be fair to require payment for land which you had no rights to before Papa and Ramón settled it."

Beaubien's grinning now. "Have you been at your grandfather's lawbooks? You have quite a sharp mind, for a mere girl."

She narrows her eyes at him, but Ramón stands and moves forward to shake Beaubien's hand, American fashion. "We will leave the matter of the documents in your hands, Don Carlos," he says. "Perhaps we may have them next week?"

The judge frowns. "It may be longer. The trials for those damn rebels will begin the Monday after Easter, which is a week from next Sunday. There will be lawyers in town then to provide legal counsel for the prisoners. One of them can draw up the correct forms." He grins at Alma. "I wouldn't want there to be any irregularities."

She smiles demurely and dips him a curtsy. A mere girl, indeed. Her mother would have had something to say about that. But she and Ramón have achieved their goal.

She looks up at the judge and finds him gazing wistfully at Andrew's averted head. She moves toward him, hands out. "Again, I want to express my deepest condolences," she says, tears springing into her eyes.

He grasps her hands and nods wordlessly.

TERESINA

CHAPTER 31 –APRIL 8 - 9, 1847
Taos, New Mexico

My mother's temper in those days was as fragile as a piece of black obsidian, and as sharp. Defiant toward the rest of the world, she wrapped herself in black and walked proudly through the streets. At home, she spoke little and seemed to prefer being alone with her ghosts: Father and Guadalupe.

We children turned elsewhere for comfort. I became my aunt's shadow, while Estefina clung to our half sister. Alfredo haunted Ceran Saint Vrain, demanding endless retellings of the fight at the pueblo.

I saw Mama's icy reserve break only once. It was the Thursday after Easter. She was preparing to attend the trial of the Indians from the pueblo. Carlos Beaubien had been to see her the night before and said she and Rumalda must testify.

My sister and Mother were both clothed in black, but my mother also wore the tápalo, the traditional long black widow's shawl, which enveloped her head, shoulders, and skirt. Rumalda helped her arrange it, then stepped back. Mother didn't move. She stared down at the cloth, her face haggard.

"I never thought I'd wear this again," she said. She looked up at Rumalda. "After your father died—" She closed her eyes and wiped at her cheeks. A shudder ran through her, fluttering the tápalo. Then she took a deep breath. "Nothing lasts forever," she murmured. She lifted her chin, took Rumalda's arm, and moved toward the door.

"Come, children," Josefa said. "Today I will teach you how to use a mano and metate to grind corn for tortillas."

"I want to go to the trial," Alfredo said.

Josefa shook her head at him. "This is hard enough for your mother. Don't make it more difficult for her."

He sighed and went to the corner of the room where three rough-stone oblong metates were lined up, each with a smaller stone, or mano, on top. He nudged the nearest one with his foot. "This is girl's work."

"Then it should be easy for you, with your strong muscles," she teased.

He rolled his eyes and we all participated half-heartedly, scraping the bulky stone manos across the corn in the indented top of the metate, attempting to grind the grain into flour. We kept up a steady stream of chatter and complaints, hoping to convince our aunt that she was distracting us as we all listened for the outer gate.

When Rumalda and Mama finally returned, Mother went straight to her room, but Rumalda stayed with us. "You will never make a good housewife," she teased Alfredo. "That corn is still much too knobbly."

He sat back on his heels and grinned at her. "It's good enough for mountain man stew."

She chuckled. "You've been talking to Saint Vrain again." Then she looked at Josefa. "There's to be a hanging tomor-

row." She made a face. "They say the jail is too full so they must execute the men they condemned yesterday."

Alfredo stopped working the grain. "Can we go?"

The two women exchanged glances. "That will be for your mother to decide," Josefa said.

"It will be gruesome," Rumalda warned. She frowned. "In my opinion, it is an event children should not attend."

His chin jutted out. "I am no child. I am ten years old."

"You must ask your mother," Josefa said. She reached for the mano in my hands. "This is really too big for your hands, pequeña, but let me show you how to hold it more easily."

Alfredo stood up. "I'm going to ask Mother." He nudged at the metate with his toe. The big stone didn't budge. "This is women's work, anyway. I don't need to know how to do it."

As he left, Rumalda leaned forward to check Estefina's work. "Nicely done," she said approvingly.

"My hands are tired," my sister said.

Rumalda and Josefa exchanged amused glances. "Shall we go for a walk?" Josefa asked.

But then my mother entered the room, Alfredo behind her, nodding at us triumphantly. He came to crouch beside me. "She said we can go!" he whispered in my ear.

Mama turned to Rumalda and my aunt. "I think los niños should see what the law does to those who harm our family," she said. Then she closed her eyes. "But I— I cannot watch." She looked at Josefa. "Will you take them?"

The two young women exchanged glances, then slowly nodded.

"Yippee!" Alfredo said.

He was quiet enough the next day, though. The gallows had been constructed in a field behind our house, so we had only to climb a ladder to our rooftop and move past the still-gaping hole in the Lashone casa to the parapet on the north side.

As we peered over it to the ground below, I spied Alma Locke and her brother, and waved vigorously. She smiled and waved back, then turned to the old man on her other side. He glanced up at the roof and politely doffed his hat to us.

"Who's that?" Estefina asked.

"He was with Señorita Alma the day Tomás Romero was captured," I told her.

"It's Ramón Chavez," Josefa said. "He is Señorita Locke's godfather."

"And all she has left of that generation," Rumalda said. "It's very sad."

"Look!" Alfredo said, pointing to our left. "Here they come!"

The prisoners came around the corner from the direction of the jail, guarded by half a dozen americano soldiers and followed by several more men who weren't in uniform. An officer sat on a horse, watching intently. The crowd below us was bigger now and spread halfway to the gallows, but no one stirred.

When the prisoners reached the place of execution, the man on the horse made a sign to someone on the platform. The gallows consisted of a wood-board platform and a hand-adzed beam mounted above it. Six rope nooses hung at carefully spaced intervals from the beam.

The guards directed the prisoners onto the platform and placed them in position, one beside each rope. The rebel at the far right end seemed very young, not much more than a boy. He had straight black hair that fell over his forehead. I frowned. He seemed familiar. I was turning to Rumalda to ask about him when Padre Martínez appeared below the platform and began moving along it, speaking to each man in turn.

One of them spat into the priest's face and lifted his head to yell "I am no traitor!" Below us, the crowd moved restlessly. The officer on the horse turned menacingly and the crowd settled.

Padre Martínez finished speaking to the last of the prisoners, made the sign of the cross, and moved away. The young man I was curious about looked at the prisoner to his right and said something, and the other held out a hand.

"Who are they?" I asked Josefa. "Those two holding hands."

She squinted, then sighed and looked sympathetically in Alma Locke's direction. "They are the Paiz brothers," she said. "Manuel Antonio and Ysidro Antonio Paiz."

I frowned. "The Manuel Antonio who was so nice to Señorita Alma at the dance at my godfather's house?"

"And his older brother. Sí." She peered at Alma again. "How can she bear it?"

Suddenly, there was a loud creaking sound from the direction of the gallows. Six sections of the platform dropped away from the prisoners' feet. They all fell into empty air.

"Oh!" Estefina gasped. She grabbed her stomach as I stared in disbelief. All the rebels' heads had snapped to one side, as if they'd been twisted right off. Some of them had their tongues out. The boy at the end still clutched the hand of the man next to him. A cheer went up from the soldiers and the men who'd followed the prisoners in.

My stomach lurched. I looked down at the crowd, searching for a place to rest my eyes. Alma Locke stood stock still, one hand over her mouth, staring at Manuel Paiz. Then she turned and pushed her way out of the crowd, her brother and Señor Chavez close behind.

I wished I was with them. Beside me, Alfredo leaned out over the parapet to get a better look while Estefina threw up in a corner. I was so glad when Josefa reached for me. "Let us go home," she whispered. "Let us go home."

ALMA

CHAPTER 32 – APRIL 9 - 10, 1847
Taos, New Mexico

When Alma, Andrew, and Ramón arrive back at the casa, they find Anamaria in the courtyard, pacing wildly, her hair in a braid down her back. "The trial, it has come," she says breathlessly. She puts her hand to her chest. "My heart has gone crazy." Then she crumples onto the bench next to the kitchen door and covers her face as she rocks back and forth. "Oh, mi hijo, my Juanito!"

Alma moves to sit beside her as the men exchange uncomfortable looks and slip past. "Will you attend?" Alma asks.

Anamaria sits up. "Am I allowed?"

"I believe so." Alma makes a face. "From what I heard at the hanging this morning—"

"Oh, my Juanito!" Anamaria covers her face again. "They will hang you!"

"They may find him not guilty."

It's clear Anamaria doesn't think this is a likely outcome. She clutches Alma's arm. "But I can attend? He can see that I am there?" Then she shudders and looks away. "I am afraid."

"I'll go with you."

"Oh, señorita!"

Alma pats her hand, remembering the long wait for news of Andrew. "It's the least I can do."

The courtroom is crowded the next morning, but when the onlookers see the two women—one the daughter and grand-daughter of men killed by the mob, the other the mother of an accused insurrecto—they make way. Alma finds herself seated on a half-empty bench near the front, apparently reserved for special guests. Anamaria touches her hair, assuring that the carefully coiled braid is secure.

The court is called to order and Judge Beaubien enters, his face pinched and tired. The prisoners are brought in, then there's a stir at the street door. Ignacia and Rumalda come down the aisle, Ignacia looking haughty, Rumalda attempting to em-ulate her mother. Josefa follows, her dark hair drawn back in a simple bun, her eyes luminous, Teresina clutching her hand. They slip in beside Alma, who greets Josefa with a smile and accepts a kiss from Teresina.

"She insisted on coming," Josefa whispers, gesturing to the child.

"At least it won't be as gruesome as the hanging yesterday," Alma murmurs.

Josefa looks at her sympathetically. "To see the Paiz broth-ers—"

Alma bites back the bile in her throat and nods. "That was difficult."

"It was awful!" Teresina says, wedging herself between the two women.

Alma gives her an amused look. "Then why did you want to come today?"

The little girl snuggles closer to her aunt. "Just because."

Josefa puts her arm around Teresina. "She has rarely left my side these two months," she tells Alma.

Anamaria has been quiet while they talked, but now she stirs. "They begin!" she hisses and Alma turns back to the housekeeper. Her eyes are fixed on her son, who looks everywhere but in his mother's direction.

The charges are read, and first Ignacia, then Rumalda, are called to tell the story of what happened the morning of January 19, 1847. Alma, who has not heard all the details, listens with growing horror. Was all the bloodshed necessary? The ferocity of the attack? She glances at Teresina, who's playing with the sash tied to Josefa's waist, her head down. To think this child saw it all.

Then the prosecutor, Francis Blair, rises from his seat. He's a small man, with a proud, freckled face and red hair. He stands firmly in front of the judge, his words sharp and to the point. Alma feels Anamaria jerk when he says them. "I charge these men with high treason!"

The young private who's acting as the prisoners' legal counsel stands up. "Your honor, I beg your pardon, but we established at the trials earlier this week that there is no legal precedent for a charge of treason. New Mexico is not officially a part of the United States of America. It is held under the rules of war, which do not allow such a charge."

Blair turns and glares at him. "Are you trying to get them off?"

Carlos Beaubien raps the table in front of him. "That will be enough, Mr. Prosecutor. The attorney for the defendants is correct. Please be so kind as to revise your plea."

Blair turns and looks at the prisoners contemptuously. "Then I charge them with murder!"

The prisoner's lawyer takes a step toward the judge. "Your honor, no one has accused these men of killing anyone or provided evidence to that effect."

Beaubien swings toward Ignacia and Rumalda. He waves a hand toward the prisoners. "Do you recall seeing any of these men at your home the morning Charles was killed?"

Ignacia turns her head, sweeping the men with her gaze. "They all look alike," she says indifferently. There's a collective gasp from the crowd.

Rumalda leans forward. "I believe what my mother means is that it was early in the morning and the lamps were not lit," she says. "Also, in the chaos, it was muy difícil to see the faces of specific individuals."

Carlos Beaubien studies her. "But you cannot say that none of these men were not present?"

She hesitates, shakes her head, then softly says, "No."

He turns to Blair. "You may proceed."

Blair swings toward the jury, which includes Benigna's husband, José Pley, and Ceran Saint Vrain. "Let the record show—" the prosecutor begins. Alma sighs and reaches for Anamaria's hand. There is nothing to do here but bear witness. She glances at the housekeeper's face. In the last ten minutes, it has aged twenty years. Her eyes do not leave her son's face.

Only when it is over does he turn to look at her, his mouth working. "¡Madre!" he calls across the courtroom.

"Be silent!" Judge Beaubien snaps. His face twists. "Did my son have the opportunity to call for his mother before you all killed him?" Then he catches himself, straightens his shoulders, and turns to the waiting crowd. "The prisoners have been found guilty and will be taken from this place to await execution on

Friday, April 30." He slams the gavel onto the table in front of him. "This court is adjourned!"

He rises and stalks out of the room. Anamaria clutches Alma's arm, but the girl's eyes follow the judge. How can he bear it?

"He should not be presiding over this trial," someone behind her says. She turns to see a young American man, perhaps seventeen, with an eager face and high forehead, staring after Beaubien. Then his gaze turns admiringly to Josefa and he bows hopefully.

Her eyes brush over him and across the crowd, then she turns to Alma with a surprised look. "Is that Rafael Luna there in the far corner?"

Alma glances across the room. Sure enough, Rafael has attended this morning's trial. There's a curvy young woman on his arm. She is quite pretty, with pale olive skin and large hazel eyes. He bends toward her, solicitously helping to arrange her rebozo.

"I thought you and he—"

Alma grins. "That was just over a month ago," she says. "I turned him down and he said he would never recover."

Josefa chortles with amusement and then catches herself and looks down at Teresina, who has buried her face in her aunt's skirts. "I want to go away from here," the little girl says.

Josefa bends toward her, eyes sober. "I as well, pequeña," she says. "Let us return to la casa."

Alma nods goodbye and turns to Anamaria, who's slumped on the bench, her face in her hands. The courtroom is emptying rapidly now and no one comes forward to greet her. "How will I bear it?" she moans.

Somehow, they make their way back to the Peabody casa, but Anamaria does not return to the kitchen. She sits on the bench in the courtyard, staring at the far wall, with Chaser at her feet. Alma does the best she can with the meal, with help from Ramón.

Andrew, too, has disappeared, but into his room. He's been like this since yesterday morning. The execution seems to have brought everything back to him. When Alma brings him a bowl of stew, he takes it listlessly.

She heads to the door, then pauses and turns back at him. "We'll go home soon," she says. "Away from all this."

He looks up at her with exhausted eyes. "I'll still see it." He points the spoon at his head. "In here."

She moves across the room and kneels beside his chair. "How can I help?"

"There's nothing anyone can do." He hands her the bowl of stew. "I can't eat this." He stares at the bed, his hands dangling in his lap.

"At least your surroundings will be different." She studies his tired face, then tries again. "You know what Mother always said. Nothing lasts forever."

He gives her a thin smile. "She wasn't always right, you know."

Alma rocks back on her heels, studying him.

He frowns. "Please don't look at me like that."

"Like what?"

"As if I'm something to be fixed." Then his frown deepens. "I'll be all right. Just go away."

"Don't you want to go home?"

He shrugs, looks at the bed again. "If you want to. It doesn't matter to me any more."

When Alma repeats this conversation to Ramón, he nods soberly. "I will approach Don Carlos once again," he says. "The lawyers are here. It is time to acquire the necessary documents."

Alma feels a stab of guilt. What of the woman sitting with vacant eyes on the bench in the courtyard? "But Anamaria—" she says.

He turns his head, studies her for a long minute, then nods. "If she wishes, she can go with us. The pass will be ready for us soon now."

Alma frowns. How does he know when Palo Flechado Pass will be safe to travel?

Two mornings later, she wakes to the sound of wind in the treetops. It's louder than the birdsong. Spring has arrived. When she ventures into the street and looks east, Alma can see that the snow on the mountain has receded up the slopes. Ramón is right. The pass home will be clear very soon now.

"Home," she murmurs. "Home!"

EPILOGUE – Fall 1847
Moreno Valley

Alma settles herself on a slab of sandstone near her grandfather's grave and rests her eyes on the valley below. There's a chill in the air. Autumn will be here soon. The aspens on the opposite slopes have brightened, ready to begin turning their vivid gold.

Andrew and Ramón are in the hay meadow, scything steadily. The activity seems to do her brother good. He's more talkative now and interested in things around him. She found him yesterday flat on his belly beside the hay meadow, watching a stream of ants prepare for winter, Chaser IV drowsing beside him.

Stands Alone's little band are still here. Two of his younger sons are turning the hay that's already cut. Alma's gaze drifts slightly south, where the band is camped on the other side of the marsh, their lodge poles stark against the pine-covered slopes of the hills. Sings Quietly and Chirping Bird move among the fires. She should go down to them.

She wonders idly what Anamaria is doing at this moment. The housekeeper had looked at Alma in horror when the girl suggested she go to the mountains with them.

"Away from my son?" she'd asked. "Who would tend to his grave?"

Two days ago, a traveler from Taos reported that the Peabody house is now locked up tight and Anamaria has gone to live at Taos Pueblo, among her dead husband's people. A man there has asked her to marry him.

The visitor also reported that Josefa and her husband are preparing to move to Rayado, south of the settlers along the Cimarron. There's a chance they'll come through this way on their journey. Teresina will be with them.

Alma smiles, glad for her friends and looking forward to seeing them. But she remains where she is, soaking in the landscape and the warmth of the rock beneath her, the comforting presence of her grandfather's grave, the touch of snow on the western mountain peaks. The sun has begun to set. She'll need to go in soon.

Then the grass behind her rustles. She turns to find Stands Alone. "Is it well with you?" he asks.

She smiles up at him. "It is well." She scoots to one side and pats the warm boulder.

He eases himself down beside her. "You speak with your ancestors?"

She glances toward her grandfather's grave and nods.

"It is good to do so." He gestures toward the valley. "And to listen to this."

She tilts her head in agreement. A meadowlark calls from the hillside behind them. A blackbird trills in the marsh. A small breeze touches Alma's forehead. She pushes a curl away from her face and gazes toward the blue mountains at the end of the valley.

"My mother once told me that nothing lasts forever," she says. She swings her head, studying the mountains, their snowy tops now touched with red-gold. "She was wrong about that."

Stands Alone nods. "This lasts," he agrees. "This land."

"My parents' land."

He shoots her a quick glance. "No man or woman owns the land."

She smiles slightly. "It owns us, I think. I meant that I feel them here. Even though they're buried in Taos, they're still part of it."

"My ancestors, also."

"Yes."

They sit for a long while, watching the sun go down, then the old man and the girl each sigh deeply, rise, and walk together down the hill.

∼ THE END ∼

NOTE TO READER

This book has been both a challenge and a joy to write. A challenge because it's a book full of grief, most of it caused by fear, greed, and ego. A joy because it's about two young women, one fictional, one historical, who refuse to let events destroy their spirit.

You can find more about Alma in my novels *No Secret Too Small,* which precedes this one, and *The Pain and the Sorrow,* where, many years later, she aids another young woman who also suffers, though in a different way, at the hands of ego and greed.

There isn't much about Teresina Bent in the historical record except what we can infer from accounts about her father. Teresina's memories served as the primary source material for everything subsequently written about her family's experiences the morning of January 19, 1847 and the following fifteen days until the American military arrived in the Taos Valley.

Teresina's accounts differed from each other, changing over time and as they were filtered through the sensibilities and needs of the reporters with whom she shared her story. I have sorted through these records and put together what appears to me to be a plausible timeline.

Lack of detail in the historical record is always a challenge. I could find no details about what was said and by whom at the April 1847 Taos trials. We do know that prosecuting attorney Francis Preston Blair, Jr. the future Missouri senator and Union general, was eager to accuse the prisoners of high treason. The charge stuck in only two cases and, even then, the U.S. Congress eventually reprimanded the Army commander in New Mexico for allowing those.

After all, New Mexico was still part of Mexico in Spring 1847. A defendant can't be guilty of treason against a country of which he or she isn't a citizen. And the U.S didn't yet own New Mexico. The war wasn't over.

New Mexican resistance to the Americans wasn't over, either. Guerrilla outbreaks continued for months after the Taos trials and only ended late that year when word arrived that the Mexican leadership had conceded defeat.

As with all my historical New Mexico fiction, I have done my best in this book to stay within the confines of the historical record while fleshing out the facts with what might have been or what could plausibly be interpolated from what we know. As a result, though the Locke family, Ramón Chavez, Jeremiah Peabody, and Anamaria Pacheco are all products of my imagination, the rest of the characters in this book are based on historical figures. You can find information about the major actors—Manuel Armijo, Padre José Antonio Martínez, Cornelio Vigil, Luis Lee, Charles Beaubien, Ceran Saint Vrain, Charles Bent, and so forth—in any book on New Mexico history.

Unfortunately, there is little information available about the major ones, people like insurrectos Manuel Antonio and Manuel Ysidro Paiz, the brothers who fought and died together. I could find little about them except their ages, where they were from, and their parents' names. Their father's name was Ysidro Romero and normally I would have used this last name for them, as well. In order to eliminate confusion with Tomas Romero, I have chosen to identify the brothers by a variant of their mother's last name (she was Matiana Perez or Paiz, depending on the source).

For more information about the events of 1846-1847 as they were experienced in Santa Fe, see my novel, *An Unhappy Country*.

FURTHER READING

These are some of the resources I accessed during my research for this novel. If you're interested in learning more about New Mexico and the Mexican American conflict, these are good starting points.

Beyreis, David. *Blood in the Borderlands: Conflict, Kinship, and the Bent Family, 1821-1920.* Lincoln, NE: University of Nebraska, 2020.

Crutchfield, James. *Revolt at Taos: The New Mexican and Indian Insurrection of 1847.* Yardley, PA: Westholme, 2015.

Durand, John. *The Taos Massacres.* Elkhorn, WI: Puzzle-box, 2004.

Gardner, Mark L. and Marc Simmons, eds. *The Mexican War Correspondence of Richard Smith Elliott.* Norman, OK: University of Oklahoma, 1997.

Garrard, Lewis H. *Wah-to-yah and the Taos Trail.* Norman, OK: University of Oklahoma, 1955.

Greenburg, Amy. *A Wicked War: Polk, Clay, Lincoln, and the 1846 U.S. Invasion of Mexico.* New York, NY: Knopf, 2012.

Keleher, William. *Turmoil in New Mexico, 1846-1848.* Santa Fe, NM: Rydale, 1952.

McNierney, Michael (ed.). *Taos 1847, The Revolt in Contemporary Accounts.* Boulder, CO: Johnson Publishing Company, 1980.

Parris, William E. *Frank Blair, Lincoln's Conservative.* Columbia, MO: University of Missouri, 1998.

Twitchell, Ralph. *The History of the Military Occupation of the Territory of New Mexico, 1846-1851.* Denver, CO: Smith-Brooks, 1909.

Vidaurre, Alberto. "1847: Revolt or Resistance." *In Taos: A Topical History*, eds. Corina A. Santistevan and Julia Moore. Santa Fe: Museum of New Mexico, 2013.

VOCABULARY

Most of the Spanish words or phrases in this novel are translated in the text or have an English cognate. The list below contains terms that don't fit either of these categories.

adobe – unburnt brick dried in the sun. Common building material in New Mexico in the 1800s.

agua – water

amante – lover

amigo/amiga – friend (male/female)

biscochitos – rolled and cut cookie flavored with anise and cinnamon

bueno – good, very well, all right

buenos días – good day/good morning

curandera – healer

Dios – God

Don – Mister, Sir. Spanish title for gentlemen which is used only before the Christian, or first, name. Used for someone with money and/or family connections

Doña – title of respect for a lady with money and/or family connections. Used only with the Christian, or first, name.

Don Fernando/Don Fernando de Taos – Over time, what is today known as the town of Taos has been called Don Fernando de Taos, San Fernando de Taos, and Fernando de Taos. In the 1800s, the First Peoples pueblo of Taos three miles northeast of the village was more likely to be called Taos. In this novel, I use Don Fernando de Taos or simply Don Fernando to refer to the village.

fanega - A measure of grain equal to 2.577 bushels, or 144 pounds. There could be some variability (1.5 to 2.5 bushels), depending on the locality.

genízaro/a - A non-Pueblo Indian captive "rescued" by Spanish settlers from the non-Christian "savage" tribes and baptized into the New Mexico communities, or a child or descendant of these captives.

madre – mother

maldicíon – damnation (as imprecation) (Spanish)

mierda – excrement (shit)

padre – father, priest

pequeña – little one

pobrecito – poor little one

por favor – please

qué – what

rebozo – a wide, long woven shawl worn by women in New Mexico and Mexico

rico – rich, opulent, wealthy

saldado – soldier

señor – Sir, mister. Also used in the sense of "gentleman."

señora – madam, lady. Also used in the sense of "gentle woman."

señorita – young lady, Miss

sí – yes

Taos – the pueblo of Taos three miles northeast of today's town of Taos.

tu – your

9 781952 026133